Back Home

Eugene Wood

Back Home

Eugene Wood

© 1st World Library – Literary Society, 2004
PO Box 2211
Fairfield, IA 52556
www.1stworldlibrary.org
First Edition

LCCN: 2004091183

Softcover ISBN: 1-59540-629-8
eBook ISBN: 1-59540-729-4

Purchase *"Back Home"*
as a traditional bound book at:
www.1stWorldLibrary.org/purchase.asp?ISBN=1-59540-629-8

1st World Library Literary Society is a nonprofit
organization dedicated to promoting literacy by:

- Creating a free internet library accessible from any computer worldwide.
- Hosting writing competitions and offering book publishing scholarships.

Readers interested in supporting literacy
through sponsorship, donations or
membership please contact:
literacy@1stworldlibrary.org
Check us out at: www.1stworldlibrary.org

Back Home

contributed by the Charles Family
in support of
1st World Library Literary Society

TO
THE SAINTED MEMORY
OF HER WHOM, IN THE DAYS BACK HOME,
I KNEW AS "MY MA MAG"
AND WHO WAS MORE TO ME THAN I CAN
TELL, EVEN
IF MY TARDY WORDS COULD REACH HER
THIS BOOK IS DEDICATED

"That she who is an angel now
Might sometimes think of me"

CONTENTS

INTRODUCTION

GENTLE READER: - Let me make you acquainted with my book, "Back Home." (Your right hand, Book, your right hand. Pity's sakes! How many times have I got to tell you that? Chest up and forward, shoulders back and down, and turn your toes out more.)

It is a little book, Gentle Reader, but please don't let that prejudice you against it. The General Public, I know, likes to feel heft in its hand when it buys a book, but I had hoped that you were a peg or two above the General Public. That mythical being goes on a reading spree about every so often, and it selects a book which will probably last out the craving, a book which "it will be impossible to lay down, after it is once begun, until it is finished." (I quote from the standard book notice). A few hours later the following dialogue ensues:

"Henry!"

"Yes, dear."

"Aren't you 'most done reading?"

"Just as soon as I finish this chapter." A sigh and a long wait.

"Henry!"

"Yes, dear."

"Did you lock the side-door?" No answer.

"Henry! Did you?"

"Did I what?"

"Did you lock the side-door?"

"In a minute now."

"Yes, but did you?"

"M-hm. I guess so."

"'Guess so!' Did you lock that side-door? They got in at Hilliard's night before last and stole a bag of clothes-pins."

"M."

"Oh, put down that book, and go and lock the side-door. I'll not get a wink of sleep this blessed night unless you do."

"In a minute now. Just wait till I finish this . . . "

"Go do it now."

Mr. General Public has a card on his desk that says, "Do it Now," and so he lays down his book with a patient sigh, and comes back to it with a patent grouch.

"Oh, so it is," says the voice from the bedroom. "I remember now, I locked it myself when I put the milkbottles out . . . . I'm going to stop taking of that man unless there's more cream on the top than there has been here lately."

"M."

"Henry!"

"Oh, what is it?"

"Aren't you 'most done reading?"

"In a minute, just as soon as I finish this chapter."

"How long is that chapter, for mercy's sakes?"

"I began another."

"Henry!"

"What?"

"Aren't you coming to bed pretty soon? You know I can't go to sleep when you are sitting up."

"Oh, hush up for one minute, can't ye? It's a funny thing if I can't read a little once in a while."

"It's a funny thing if I've got to be broke of my rest this way. As much as I have to look after. I'd hate to be so selfish . . . . Henry! Won't you please put the book down and come to bed?"

"Oh, for goodness sake! Turn over and go to sleep. You make me tired."

Every two or three hours Mrs. General Public wakes up and announces that she can't get a wink of sleep, not a wink; she wishes he hadn't brought the plagued old book home; he hasn't the least bit of consideration for her; please, please, won't he put the book away and come to bed?

He reaches "THE END" at 2:30A.M., turns off the gas, and creeps into bed, his stomach all upset from smoking so much without eating anything, his eyes feeling like two burnt holes in a blanket, and wishing that he had the sense he was born with. He'll have to be up at 6:05, and he knows how he will feel. He also knows how he will feel along about three o'clock in the afternoon. Smithers is coming then to close up that deal. Smithers is as sharp as tacks, as slippery as an eel, and as crooked as a dog's hind leg. Always looking for the best of it. You need all your wits when you deal with Smithers. Why didn't he take Mrs. General Public's advice, and get to bed instead of sitting up fuddling himself with that fool love-story?

That's how a book should be to be a great popular success, and one that all the typewriter girls will have on their desks. I am guiltily conscious that "Back Home" is not up to standard either in avoirdupois heft or the power to unfit a man for business.

Here's a book. Is it long? No. Is it exciting? No. Any lost diamonds in it? Nup. Mysterious murders? No. Whopping big fortune, now teetering this way, and now teetering that, tipping over on the Hero at the last and smothering him in an avalanche of fifty-dollar bills? No. Does She get Him? Isn't even that. No "heart interest" at all. What's the use of putting out good money to make such a book; to have a cover design for

Eugene Wood

it; to get a man like A. B. Frost to draw illustrations for it, when he costs so like the mischief, when there's nothing in the book to make a man sit up till 'way past bedtime? Why print it at all?

You may search me. I suppose it's all right, but if it was my money, I'll bet I could make a better investment of it. If worst came to worst, I could do like the fellow in the story who went to the gambling-house and found it closed up, so he shoved the money under the door and went away. He'd done his part.

And yet, on the other hand, I can see how some sort of a case can be made out for this book of mine. I suppose I am wrong - I generally am in regard to everything - but it seems to me that quite a large part of the population of this country must be grown-up people. If I am right in this contention, then this large part of the population is being unjustly discriminated against. I believe in doing a reasonable amount for the aid and comfort of the young things that are just beginning to turn their hair up under, or who rub a stealthy forefinger over their upper lips to feel the pleasant rasp, but I don't believe in their monopolizing everything. I don't think it's fair. All the books printed - except, of course, those containing valuable information; we don't buy those books, but go to the public library for them - all the books printed are concerned with the problem of How She can get Him, and He can get Her.

Well, now. It was either yesterday morning or the day before that you looked in the glass and beheld there The First Gray Hair. You smiled a smile that was not all pure pleasure, a smile that petered out into a sigh, but nevertheless a smile, I will contend. What do you think about it? You're still on earth, aren't you? You'll last the month out, anyhow, won't you? Not at all ready to be laid on the shelf? What do you think of the relative importance of Love, Courtship, and Marriage? One or two other things in life just about as interesting, aren't there? Take getting a living, for instance. That 's worthy of one's attention, to a certain extent. When our young ones ask us: "Pop, what did you say to Mom when you courted her?" they feel provoked at us for taking it so lightly and so frivolously. It vexes them for us to reply: "Law, child! I don't remember. Why, I says to her: 'Will you have me?" And she says: 'Why, yes, and jump at the chance.'" What difference does it make what we said, or whether we said anything at all? Why should we charge our memories with the recollections of those few and foolish months of mere instinctive sex-attraction when all that really counts came after, the years wherein low passion blossomed into lofty Love, the dear companionship in joy and sorrow, and in that which is more, far more than either joy or sorrow, "the daily round, the common task?" All that is wonderful to think of in our courtship is the marvel, for which we should never cease to thank the Almighty God, that with so little judgment at our disposal we should have chosen so wisely.

If you, Gentle Reader, found your first gray hair day before yesterday morning, if you can remember, 'way, 'way back ten or fifteen years ago . . . er . . . er . . . or more, come with me. Let us go "Back Home." Here's your transportation, all made out to you, and in your hand. It is no use my reminding you that no railroad goes to the old home place. It isn't there any more, even in outward seeming. Cummins's woods, where you had your robbers' cave, is all cleared off and cut up into building lots. The cool and echoing covered bridge, plastered with notices of dead and forgotten Strawberry Festivals and Public Vendues, has long ago been torn down to be replaced by a smart, red iron bridge. The Volunteer Firemen's Engine-house, whose brick wall used to flutter with the gay rags of circus-bills, is gone as if it never were at all. Where the Union Schoolhouse was is all torn up now. They are putting up a new magnificent structure, with all the modern improvements, exposed plumbing, and spankless discipline. The quiet leafy streets echo to the hissing snarl of trolley cars, and the power-house is right by the Old Swimming-hole above the dam. The meeting-house, where we attended Sabbath-school, and marveled at the Greek temple frescoed on the wall behind the pulpit, is now a church with a big organ, and stained-glass windows, and folding opera-chairs on a slanting floor. There isn't any "Amen Corner," any more, and in these calm and well-bred times nobody ever gets "shouting happy."

But even when "the loved spots that our infancy knew" are physically the same, a change has come upon them more saddening than words can tell. They have shrunken and grown shabbier. They are not nearly so spacious and so splendid as once they were.

Some one comes up to you and calls you by your name. His voice echoes in the chambers of your memory. You hold his hand in yours and try to peer through the false-face he has on, the mask of a beard or spectacles, or a changed expression of the counte-nance. He says he is So-and-so. Why, he used to sit with you in Miss Crutcher's room, don't you remember? There was a time when you and he walked together, your arms upon each other's shoulders. But this is some other one than he. The boy you knew had freckles, and could spit between his teeth, ever and ever so far.

They don't have the same things to eat they used to have , or , if they do , it all tastes different. Do you remember the old well, with the windlass and the chain fastened to the rope just above the bucket, the chain that used to cluck-cluck when the dripping bucket came within reach to be swung upon the well-curb? How cold the water used to be, right out of the northwest corner of the well! It made the roof of your mouth ache when you drank. Everybody said it was such splendid water. It isn't so very cold these days , and I think it has a sort of funny taste to it.

Ah, Gentle Reader, this is not really "Back Home" we gaze upon when we go there by the train. It is a last year's bird's nest. The nest is there; the birds are flown, the birds of youth, and noisy health, and ravenous appetite, and inexperience. You cannot go "Back Home" by train, but here is the magic wishing-carpet, and here is your transportation in your hand all made out to you. You and I will make the journey together. Let us in heart and mind thither ascend.

I went to the Old Red School-house with you. Don't you remember me? I was learning to swim when you could go clear across the river without once "letting down." I saw you at the County Fair, and bought a slab of ice-cream candy just before you did. I was in the infant-class in Sabbath-school when you spoke in the dialogue at the monthly concert. Look again. Don't you remember me? I used to stub my toe so; you ought to recollect me by that. I know plenty of people that you know. I may not always get their names just right, but then it's been a good while ago. You ll recognize them, though; you'll know them in a minute.

EUGENE WOOD.

THE OLD RED SCHOOL-HOUSE

Oh, the little old red school-house on the hill,
(2d bass: On the hill.)
Oh, the little old red school-house on the hill,
(2d bass: On the hi-hi-hi-yull)
And my heart with joy o'erflows,
Like the dew-drop in the rose,*
Thinking of the old red SCHOOL-HOUSE
I o-o-on the hill,
(2d tenor and 1st bass: The hill, the hill.)

THE MALE QUARTET'S COMPENDIUM.

* I call your attention to the chaste beauty of this line, and the imperative necessity of the chord of the diminished seventh for the word "rose." Also "school-house" in the last line must be very loud and staccato. Snap it off.

If the audience will kindly come forward and occupy the vacant seats in the front of the hall, the entertainment will now begin. The male quartet will first render an appropriate selection and then . . . . Can't you see them from where you are? Let me assist you in the visualization.

The first tenor, the gentleman on the extreme left, is a

stocky little man, with a large chest and short legs conspicuously curving inward. He has plenty of white teeth, ash-blonde hair, and goes smooth-shaven for purely personal reasons. His round, dough-colored face will never look older (from a distance) than it did when he was nine. The flight of years adds only deeper creases in the multitude of fine wrinkles, and increasing difficulty in hoisting his tiny, patent-leather foot up on his plump knee.

The second tenor leans toward him in a way to make another man anxious about his watch, but the second tenor is as honest as the day. He is only "blending the voices." He works in the bank. He is going to be married in June sometime. Don't look around right away, but she's the one in the pink shirt-waist, the second one from the aisle, the one . . . two . . . three . . . the sixth row back. See her? Say, they've got it bad, those two. What d' ye think? She goes down by the bank every day at noon, so as to walk up with him to luncheon. She lives across the street, and as soon as ever she has finished her luncheon, there she is, out on the front porch hallooing: "Oo-hoo!" How about that? And if he so much as looks at another girl - m-M!

The first bass is one of these fellows with a flutter in his voice. No, I don't mean a vibrato. It's a flutter, like a goat's tail. It is considered real operatic.

The second bass has a great, big Adam's apple that slides up and down his throat like a toy-monkey on a stick. He is tall, and has eyebrows like clothes-brushes, and he scowls fit to make you run and hide under the bed. He is really a good-hearted fellow, though. Pity he has the dyspepsia so bad. Oh, my, yes! Suffers everything with it, poor man. He generally sings that song about "Drink-ing! DRINK-ang! Drink-awng!" though he's strictly temperate himself. When he takes that last low note, you hold on to your chair for fear you'll fall in too.

But why bring in the male quartet?

Because "The Little Old Red School-house" is more than a mere collocation of words, accurately descriptive. It is what Mat King would call a "symblem," and as such requires the music's dying fall to lull and enervate a too meticulous and stringent tendency to recollect that it wasn't little, or old, or red, or on a hill. It might have been big and new, and built of yellow brick, right next to the Second Presbyterian, and hence close to the "branch," so that the spring freshets flooded the playground, and the water lapped the base of the big rock on which we played "King on the Castle," - the big rock so pitifully dwindled of late years. No matter what he facts are. Sing 'of "The Little Old Red Schoolhouse On the Hill" and in everybody's heart a chord trembles in unison. As we hear its witching strains, we are all lodge brethren, from Maine to California and far across the Western Sea; we are all lodge brethren, and the air is "Auld Lang Syne," and we are clasping hands across, knitted together into one living solidarity; and this, if we but sensed it, is the real Union, of which the federal compact is but the outward seeming. It is a Union in which they have neither art nor part whose parents sent them to private schools, so as not to have them associate with "that class of people." It is the true democracy which batters down the walls that separate us from each other - the walls of caste distinction, and color prejudice, and national hatred, and religious contempt, all the petty, anti-social meannesses that quarrel with

"The Union of hearts, the Union of hands,
And the flag of our Union forever."

Old Glory has floated victoriously on many a gallant fight by sea and land, but never do its silver stars glitter more bravely or its blood-red stripes curve more proudly on the fawning breeze than when it floats above the school-house, over the daily battle against ignorance and prejudice (which is ignorance of our fellows), for freedom and for equal rights. It is no mere pretty sentimentality that puts the flag there, but the serious recognition of the bed-rock principle of our Union: That we are all of one blood, one bounden duty; that all these anti-social prejudices are just as shameful as illiteracy, and that they must disappear as soon as ever we shall come to know each other well. Knowledge is power. That is true. And it is also true: A house divided against itself cannot stand.

"The Flag of our Union forever!" is our prayer, our heart's desire for us and for our children after us. Heroes have died to give us that, heroes that with glazing eyes beheld the tattered ensign and spent their latest breath to cheer it as it passed on to triumph. "We who are about to die salute thee!" The heart swells to think of it. But it swells, too, to think that, day by day, thousands upon thousands of little children stretch out their hands toward that Flag and pledge allegiance to it. "We who are about to LIVE salute thee!"

It is no mere chance affair that all our federal buildings should be so ugly and so begrudged, and that our school-houses should be so beautiful architecturally - the one nearest my house is built from plans that took the first prize at the Paris Exposition, in competition with the whole world - so well-appointed, and so far from being grudged that the complaint is, that there are not enough of them.

That So-and-so should be the President, and such-and-such a party have control is but a game we play at, amateurs and professionals; the serious business is, that in this country no child, how poor soever it may be, shall have the slightest let or hindrance in the equal chance with every other child to learn to read, and write, and cipher, and do raffia-work.

It is a new thing with us to have splendid school-houses. After all, the norm, as you might say, is still "The Old Red School-house." You must recollect how hard the struggle is for the poor farmer, with wheat only a dollar a bushel, and eggs only six for a quarter; with every year or so taxes of three and sometimes four dollars on an eighty-acre farm grinding him to earth. It were folly to expect more in rural districts than a tight box, with benches and a stove in it. Never-the-less, it is the thing signified more than its outward seeming that catches and holds the eye upon the country school-house as you drive past it. You count yourself fortunate if, mingled with the creaking of the buggy-springs, you hear the hum of recitation; yet more fortunate if it is recess time, and you can see the children out at play, the little girls holding to one another's dress-tails as they solemnly circle to the chant:

"H-yar way gow rand tha malbarry bosh,
Tha malbarry bosh, tha malbarry bosh,
H-yar way gow rand tha malbarry bosh
On a cay-um and frasty marneng."

The boys are at marbles, if it is muddy enough, or

one-old-cat, or pom-pom-peel-away, with the normal percentage of them in reboant tears - that is to say, one in three.

But even this is not the moment of illumination, when it comes upon you like a flood how glorious is the land we live in, upon what sure and certain footing are its institutions, when we know by spiritual insight that whatsoever be the trial that awaits us, the people of these United States, we shall be able for it! Yes. We shall be able for it.

If you would learn the secret of our nation's greatness, take your stand some winter's morning just before nine o'clock, where you can overlook a circle of some two or three miles' radius, the center being the Old Red School-house. You will see little figures picking their way along the miry roads, or ploughing through the deep drifts, cutting across the fields, all drawing to the school-house, Bub in his wammus and his cowhide boots, his cap with ear-laps, a knitted comforter about his neck, and his hands glowing in scarlet mittens; and little Sis, in a thick shawl, trudging along behind him, stepping in his tracks. They chirrup, "Good-morning, sir!" As far as you can see them you have to watch them, and something rises in your throat. Lord love 'em! Lord love the children!

And then it comes to you, and it makes you catch your breath to think of it, that every two or three miles all over this land, wherever there are children at all, there is the Old Red Schoolhouse. At this very hour a living tide, upbearing the hopes and prayers of God alone knows how many loving hearts, the tide on which all of our longed-for ships are to come in, is setting to the school-house. Oh, what is martial glory, what is

Eugene Wood

conquest of an empire, what is state-craft alongside of this? Happy is the people that is in such a case!

The city schools are now the pattern for the country schools: but in my day, although a little they were pouring the new wine of frothing educational reform into the old bottles, they had not quite attained the full distention of this present. We still had some kind of a good time, but nothing like the good times they had out at the school near grandpap's, where I sometimes visited. There you could whisper! Yes, sir, you could whisper. So long as you didn't talk out loud, it was all right. And there was no rising at the tap of the bell, forming in line and walking in lock-step. Seemingly it never entered the school-board's heads that anybody would ever be sent to state's prison. They left the scholars unprepared for any such career. They have remedied all that in city schools. Now, when a boy grows up and goes to Sing Sing, he knows exactly what to do and how to behave. It all comes back to him.

But what I call the finest part of going to school in the country was, that you didn't go home to dinner. Grandma had a boy only a few years older than I was, and when I went a-visiting, she fixed us up a "piece." They call it "luncheon" now, I think - a foolish, hybrid mongrel of a word, made up of "lump," a piece of bread, and "noon," and "shenk," a pouring or drink. But the right name is "piece." What made this particular "piece" taste so wonderfully good was that it was in a round-bottomed basket woven of splints dyed blue, and black and red, and all in such a funny pattern. It was an Indian basket. My grandma's mother, when she was a little girl, got that from the squaw of old Chief Wiping-Stick.

The "piece" had bread-and-butter (my grandma used to let me churn for her sometimes, when I went out there), and some of the slices had apple-butter on them. (One time she let me stir the cider, when it was boiling down in the big kettle over the chunk-fire out in the yard. The smoke got in my eyes.) Sometimes there was honey from the hives over by the gooseberry bushes - the gooseberries had stickers on them - and we had slices of cold, fried ham. (I was out at grandpap's one time when they butchered. They had a chunk-fire then, too, to heat the water to scald the hogs. And say! Did your grandma ever roast pig's tails in the ashes for you?) And there were crullers. No, I don't mean "doughnuts." I mean crullers, all twisted up. They go good with cider. (Sometimes my grandma cut out thin, pallid little men of cruller dough, and dropped them into the hot lard for my Uncle Jimmy and me. And when she fished them out, they were all swelled up and "pussy," and golden brown.

And there was pie. Neither at the school nooning nor at the table did one put a piece of pie upon a plate and haggle at it with a fork. You took the piece of pie up in your hand and pointed the sharp end toward you, and gently crowded it into your face. It didn't require much pressure either.

And there were always apples, real apples. I think they must make apples in factories nowadays. They taste like it. These were real ones, picked off the trees. Out at grandpap's they had bellflowers, and winesaps, and seek-no-furthers, and, I think, sheep-noses, and one kind of apple that I can't find any more, though I have sought it carefully. It was the finest apple I ever set a tooth in. It was the juiciest and the spiciest apple. It had sort of a rollicking flavor to it, if you know what I mean. It certainly was the ne plus ultra of an apple. And the name of it was the rambo. Dear me, how good it was! think I'd sooner have one right now than great riches. And all these apples they kept in the apple-hole. You went out and uncovered the earth and there they were, all in a big nest of straw; and such a gush of perfume distilled from that pile of them that just to recollect it makes my mouth all wet.

They had a big red apple in those days that I forget the name of. Oh, it was a whopper! You'd nibble at it and nibble at it before you could get a purchase on it. Then, after you got your teeth in, you'd pull and pull, and all of a sudden the apple would go "tock!" and your head would fly back from the recoil, and you had a bite about the size of your hand. You "chomped" on it, with your cheek all bulged out, and blame near drowned yourself with the juice of it.

Noon-time the girls used to count the seeds:

"One I love, two I love, three my love I see;
Four I love with all my heart, and five I cast away.
Six he loves; seven she loves; eight . . . eight . . . "

I forget what eight is, and all that follows after. And then the others would tease her with, "Aw, Jennie!" knowing who it was she had named the apple for, Wes. Rinehart, or 'Lonzo Curl, or whoever. And you'd be standing there by the stove, kind of grinning and not thinking of anything in particular when somebody would hit you a clout on your back that just about broke you in two, and would tell you "to pass it on," and you'd pass it on, and the next thing was you'd think the house was coming down. Such a chasing around and over benches, and upsetting the water-bucket, and tearing up Jack generally that teacher would say, "Boys! boys! If you can't play quietly, you'll have to go out of doors!" Play quietly! Why, the idea! What kind of play is it when you are right still?

Outdoors in the country, you can whoop and holler, and carry on, and nobody complains to the board of health. And there are so many things you can do. If there is just the least little fall of snow you can make a big wheel, with spokes in it, by your tracking. I remember that it was called "fox and geese," but that's all I can remember about it. If there was a little more snow you tried to wash the girls' faces in it, and sometimes got yours washed. If there was a good deal of wet snow you had a snowball fight, which is great fun, unless you get one right smack dab in your ear - oh, but I can't begin to tell you all the fun there is at the noon hour in the country school, that the town children don't know anything about. And when it was time for school to "take up," there wasn't any forming in line, with a monitor to run tell teacher who snatched off Joseph Humphreys' cap and flung it far away, so he had to get out of the line, and who did this, and who did that - no penitentiary business at all. Teacher tapped on the window with a ruler, and the boys and girls came in, red-faced and puffing, careering through the aisles, knocking things off the desks with many a burlesque, "oh, exCUSE me!" and falling into their seats, bursting into sniggers, they didn't know what at. They had an hour and a half nooning. Counting that it took five minutes to shovel down even grandma's beautiful "piece," that left an hour and twenty-five minutes for roaring, romping play. If you want to know, I think that is fully as educational and a far better preparation for life than sitting still with your nose stuck in a book.

In the city schools they don't think so. Even the stingy fifteen minutes' recess, morning and afternoon, has been stolen from the children. Instead is given the inspiriting physical culture, all making silly motions together in a nice, warm room, full of second-hand air. Is it any wonder that one in every three that die between fifteen and twenty-five, dies of consumption?

You must have noticed that almost everybody that amounts to anything spent his early life in the country. The city schools have great educational advantages; they have all the up-to-date methods, but the output of the Old Red Schoolhouse compares very favorably with that of the city schools for all that. The two-mile walk, morning and evening, had something to do with it, not only because it and the long nooning were good exercise, but because it impressed upon the mind that what cost so much effort to get must surely be worth having. But I think I know another reason.

If the city child goes through the arithmetic once, it is as much as ever. In the Old Red School-house those who hadn't gone through the arithmetic at least six times, were little thought of. In town, the last subject in the book was "Permutation," to which you gave the mere look its essentially frivolous nature deserved. It was: "End of the line. All out!" But in the country a very important department followed. It was called "Problems." They were twisters, able to make "How old is Ann?" look like a last year's bird's nest. They make a big fuss about the psychology of the child's mind nowadays. Well, I tell you they couldn't teach the man that got up that arithmetic a thing about the operation of the child's mind. He knew what was what. He didn't put down the answers. He knew that if he did, weak, erring human nature, tortured by suspense, determined to have the agony over, would multiply by four and divide by thirteen, and subtract 127 - didn't, either. I didn't say "substract." I guess I know they'd get the answer somehow, it didn't matter much how.

In the country they ciphered through this part, and handed in their sums to Teacher, who said she'd take 'em home and look 'em over; she didn't have time just then. As if that fooled anybody! She had a key! And when you had done the very last one on the very last page, and there wasn't anything more except the blank pages, where you had written, "Joe Geiger loves Molly Meyers, "and," If my name you wish to see, look on page 103," and all such stuff, then you turned over to the beginning, where it says, "Arithmetic is the science of numbers, and the art of computing by them," and once more considered, "Ann had four apples and her brother gave her two more. How many did she then have?" There were the four apples in a row, and the two apples, and you that had worried over meadows so long and so wide, and men mowing them in so many days and a half, had to think how many apples Ann really did have. Some of the fellows with forked hairs on their chins and uncertain voices - the big fellows in the back seats, where the apple-cores and the spit-balls come from knew every example in the book by heart.

And there is yet another reason why the country school has brought forth men of whom we do well to be proud. At the county-seat, every so often, the school commissioners held an examination. Thither resorted many, for the most part anxious to determine if they really knew as much as they thought they did. If you took that examination and got a "stiff kit" for eighteen months, you had good cause to hold your head up and step as high as a blind horse. A "stiff kit" for eighteen months is no small thing, let me tell you. I don't know if there is anything corresponding to a doctor's hood for such as win a certificate to teach school for two years hand-running; but there ought to be. A fellow ought not to be obliged to resort to such tactics as taking out a folded paper and perusing it in the hope that some one will ask him: "What you got there, Calvin?" so as to give you a chance to say, carelessly, "Oh, jist a 'stiff-kit' for two years."

(When you get as far along as that, you simply have to take a term in the junior Prep. Department at college, not because there is anything left for you to learn, but for the sake of putting a gloss on your education, finishing it off neatly.)

And then if you were going to read law with Mr. Parker, or study medicine with old Doc. Harbaugh, and you kind of run out of clothes, you took that certificate and hunted up a school and taught it. Sometimes they paid you as high as $20 a month and board, lots of board, real buckwheat cakes ("riz" buckwheat, not the prepared kind), and real maple syrup, and real sausage, the kind that has sage in it; the kind that you can't coax your butcher to sell you. The pale, tasteless stuff he gives you for sausage I wouldn't throw out to the chickens. Twenty dollars a month and board! That's $4 a month more than a hired man gets.

But it wasn't alone the demonstration that, strange as it might seem, it was possible for a man to get his living by his wits (though that has done much to produce great men) as it was the actual exercise of teaching. Remember the big boys on the back seats, where the apple-cores and the spit-balls come from. The school-director that hired you gave you a searching look-over and said: "M-well-l-l, I'm afraid you haint hardly qualified for our school - oh, that's all right, sir; that's all right. Your 'stiff-kit' is first-rate, and you got good recommends, good recommends; but I was thinkin' - well, I tell you. Might's well out with it first as last. I d' know's I ort to say so, but this here district No. 34 is a poot' tol'able hard school to teach. Ya-uss. A poot-ty tol'able hard school to teach. Now, that's jist the plumb facts in the matter. We've had four try it this winter a'ready. One of 'em stuck it out four weeks - I jimminy! he had grit, that feller had. The balance of 'em didn't take so long to make up their minds. Well, now, if you're a mind to try it - I was goin' to say you didn't look to me like you had the heft.

Like to have you the worst way. Now, if you want to back out . . . .Well, all right. Monday mornin', eh? Well, you got my sympathies."

I believe that some have tried to figure out that St. Martin of Tours, ought to be the patron saint of the United States. One of his feast-days falls on July 4, and his colors are red, white and blue. But I rather prefer, myself, the Boanerges, the two sons of Zebedee. When asked: "Are ye able to drink of this cup?" they answered: "We are able." They didn't in the least know what it was; but they knew they were able for anything that anybody else was, and, perhaps, able for a little more. At any rate, they were willing to chance it. That's the United States of America, clear to the bone and back again to the skin.

You ask any really great man: "Have you ever taught a winter term in a country school?" If he says he hasn't, then depend upon it he isn't a really great man. People only think he is. The winter term breeds

Boanerges - sons of thunder. Yes, and of lightning, too. Something struck the big boys in the back seats, as sure as you're a foot high; and if it wasn't lightning, what was it? Brute strength for brute strength, they were more than a match for Teacher. It was up to him. It was either prove himself the superior power, or slink off home and crawl under the porch.

The curriculum of the Old Red School-house, which was, until lately, the universal curriculum, consisted in reading, writing, and arithmetic or ciphering. I like the word "ciphering," because it makes me think of slates - slates that were always falling on the floor with a rousing clatter, so that almost always at least one corner was cracked. Some mitigation of the noise was gained by binding the frame with strips of red flannel, thus adding warmth and brightness to the color scheme. Just as some fertile brain conceived the notion of applying a knob of rubber to each corner, slates went out, and I suppose only doctors buy them nowadays to hang on the doors of their offices. Maybe the teacher's nerves were too highly strung to endure the squeaking of gritty pencils, but I think the real reason for their banishment is, that slates invited too strongly the game of noughts and crosses, or tit-tat-toe, three in a row, the champion of indoor sports, and one entirely inimical to the study of the joggerfy lesson. But if slates favored tit-tat-toe, they also favored ciphering, and nothing but good can come from that. Paper is now so cheap that you need not rub out mistakes, but paper and pencil can never surely ground one in "the science of numbers and the art of computing by them." What is written is written, and returns to plague the memory, but if you made a mistake on the slate, you could spit on it and rub it out with your sleeve and leave no trace of the error, either on the writing surface or the tables of the memory. What does the hymn say?

"Forget the steps already trod,
And onward urge thy way."

The girls used to keep a little sponge and some water in a discarded patchouli bottle with a glass stopper, to wash their slates with; but it always seemed to me that the human and whole-hearted way was otherwise.

Reading, writing, and arithmetic, - these three; and the greatest of these three is arithmetic. Over against it stands grammar, which may be said to be derived from reading and writing. Show me a man that, as a boy at school, excelled in arithmetic and I will show you a useful citizen, a boss in his own business, a leader of men; show me the boy that preferred grammar, that read expressively, that wrote a beautiful hand and curled his capital S's till their tails looked like mainsprings, and I will show you a dreamer and a sentimentalist - a man that works for other people. While I have breath in me, I will maintain the supereminence of arithmetic. There is no room for disputation in arithmetic, no exceptions to the rule. Twice two is four, and that's all there is about it: but whether there be pronunciations, they shall cease; whether there be rules of grammar, they shall vanish away. Why, look here. It's a rule of grammar, isn't it, that the subject of a sentence must be put in the nominative case? Let it kick and bite, and hang on to the desks all it wants to, in it goes and the door is slammed on it. You think so? What is the word "you?" Second person, plural number, objective case. Oh, no; the nominative form is "ye."

Eugene Wood

Don't you remember it says: "Woe unto you, ye lawyers"? Those who fight against: "Him and me went down town," fight against the stars in their courses, for the objective case in every language is bound and determined to be The Whole Thing. Arithmetic alone is founded on a rock. All else is fleeting, all else is futile, chaotic - a waste of time. What is reading but a rival of morphine? There are probably as many men in prison, sent there by Reading, as by Rum.

"Oh, not good Reading!" says the publisher.

"Not good Rum, either," says the publican.

Fight it out. It's an even thing between the two of you; Literature and Liquor, Books and Booze, which can take a man's mind off his business most effectually.

Still, merely as a matter of taste, I will defend the quality of McGuffey's School Readers against all comers. I don't know who McGuffey was; but certainly he formed the greatest intellects of our age, present company not excepted. The true test of literature is its eternal modernity. A thing of beauty is a joy forever. It always seems of the age in which it is read. Now, almost the earliest lection in McGuffey's First Reader goes directly to the heart of one of the greatest of modern problems. It does not palter or beat about the bush. It asks right out, plump and plain: "Ann, how old are you?"

Year by year, until we reached the dizzy height of the Sixth Reader, were presented to us samples of the best English ever written. If you can find, up in the garret, a worn and frayed old Reader, take it down and turn its pages over. See if anything in these degenerate days compares in vital strength and beauty with the story of the boy that climbed the Natural Bridge, carving his steps in the soft limestone with his pocket knife. You cannot read it without a thrill. The same inspired hand wrote "The Blind Preacher," and who that ever can read it can forget the climax reached in that sublime line: "Socrates died like a philosopher, but Jesus Christ like a god!"

Not long ago I walked among the graves in that spot opposite where Wall Street slants away from Broadway, and my feet trod on ground worth, in the market, more than the twenty-dollar gold pieces that would cover it. My eye lighted upon a flaking brownstone slab, that told me Captain Michael Cresap rested there. Captain Michael Cresap! The intervening years all fled away before me, and once again my boyish heart thrilled with that incomparable oration in McGuffey's Reader, "Who is there to mourn for Logan? Not one." Captain Cresap was the man that led the massacre of Logan's family.

And there was more than good literature in those Readers. There was one piece that told about a little boy alone upon a country road at night. The black trees groaned and waved their skinny arms at him. The wind-torn clouds fitfully let a pale and watery moonlight stream a little through. It was very lonely. Over his shoulder the boy saw indistinct shapes that followed after, and hid themselves whenever he looked squarely at them. Then, suddenly, he saw before him in the gloom, a gaunt white specter waiting for him - waiting to get him, its arms spread wide out in menace. He was of our breed, though, this boy. He did not turn and run. With God knows what terror knocking at his ribs, he trudged ahead to meet his fate, and lo! the grisly specter proved to be a friendly guide-post to show the way that he should walk in. Brother (for you are my kin that went with me to public school, in the life that you have lived since you first read the story of Harry and the Guide-post, has it been an idle tale, or have you, too, found that what we dreaded most, what seemed to us so terrible in the future has, after all, been a friendly guide-post, showing us the way that we should walk in?

McGuffey had a Speller, too. It began with simple words in common use, like a-b ab, and e-b eb, and i-b, ib, proceeding by gradual, if not by easy stages to honorificatudinibility and disproportionableness, with a department at the back devoted to twisters like phthisic, and mullein-stalk, and diphtheria, and gneiss. We used to have a fine old sport on Friday afternoons, called "choose-up-and-spell-down." I don't know if you ever played it. It was a survival, pure and simple, from the Old Red School-house. There was where it really lived. There was where it flourished as a gladiatorial spectacle. The crack spellers of District Number 34 would challenge the crack spellers of the Sinking Spring School. The whole countryside came to the school-house in wagons at early candle-lighting time, and watched them fight it out. The interest grew as the contest narrowed down, until at last there were the two captains left - big John Rice for District Number 34, and that wiry, nervous, black-haired girl of 'Lias Hoover's, Polly Ann. She married a man by the name of Brubaker. I guess you didn't know him. His folks moved here from Clarke County. Polly Ann's eyes glittered like a snake's, and she kept putting her knuckles up to the red spots in her cheeks that burned like fire. Old John, he didn't seem to care a cent. And what do you think Polly Ann missed on? "Feoffment."

A simple little word like "feoffment!" She hadn't got further than pheph - " when she knew that she was wrong, but Teacher had said "Next!" and big John took it and spelled it right. She had a fit of nervous crying, and some were for giving her the victory, after all, because she was a lady. But big John said: "She missed, didn't she? Well. And I spelled it right, didn't I? Well. She took her chances same as the rest of us. 'Taint me you got to consider, it's District Number 34. And furthermore. AND FURTHERMORE. Next time somebuddy asts her to go home with him from singin'-school, mebby she won't snigger right in his face, and say 'No! 's' loud 'at everybuddy kin hear it."

It's quite a thing to be a good speller, but there are people who can spell any word that ever was, and yet if you should ask them right quick how much is seven times eight, they'd hem and haw and say: "Seven tums eight? Why - ah, lemme see now. Seven tums - what was it you said? Oh, seven tums eight. Why - ah, seven tums eight is sixty-three - fifty-six I mean." There's nothing really to spelling. It's just an idiosyncrasy. If there was really anything useful in it, you could do it by machinery - just the same as you can add by machinery, or write with a typewriter, or play the piano with one of these things with cut paper in it. Spelling is an old-fashioned, hand-powered process, and as such doomed to disappear with the march of improvement.

One Friday afternoon we chose up and spelled down, and the next Friday afternoon we spoke pieces. Doubtless this accounts for our being a nation of orators. I am far from implying or seeming to imply that this is anything to brag of. Anybody that can be influenced by a man with a big mouth, a loud voice, and a rush of words to the face - well, I've got my opinion of all such.

Oratory and poetry - all foolishness, I say. Better far are drawing-lessons, and raffia-work, and clay-modeling than: "I come not here to talk," and "A soldier of the Legion lay dying at Algiers," and "Old Ironsides at anchor lay." (I observe that these lines are more or less familiar to you, and that you are eager to add selections to the list, all of them known to me as well as you.) That children, especially boys, loathe to speak a piece is a fact profoundly significant. They know it is nothing in the world but foolishness; and if there is one thing above another that a child hates, it is to be made a fool in public. That's what makes them work their fingers so, and gulp, and stammer, and tremble at the knees. That is what sends them to their seats, after all is over, mad as hornets. This is something that I know about. It happened that, instead of getting funny pieces to recite as I wanted to, discerning that one silly turn deserves another, my parents, well-meaning in their way, taught me solemn things about: "O man immortal, live for something!" and all such, and I had to humiliate myself by disgorging them in public. The consequence was, that not only on Friday afternoons but whenever anybody came to visit the school, I was butchered to make a Roman holiday. Teacher was so proud of me, and the visitors let on that they were tickled half to death, but I knew better. I could see the other scholars look at one another, as much as to say: "Well, if you'll tell me why!" Even in my shame and anger I could see that. But there is one happy memory of a Friday afternoon. Determined to show my friends and fellow-citizens that I, too, was born in Arcadia, and was a living , human boy , I announced to Teacher: "I got another piece."

"Oh, have you?" cried she, sure of an extra O-man-immortal intellectual treat. "Let us hear it, by all means."

Whereupon I marched up to the platform and declaimed that deathless lyric:

"When I was a boy, I was a bold one. My mammy made me a new shirt out o' dad's old one."

All of it? Certainly. Isn't that enough? That was the only distinctly popular platform effort I ever made. I am proud of it now. I was proud of it then. But the news of my triumph was coldly received at home.

I don't know whether it has since gone out of date, but in my day and time a very telling feature of school exhibitions was reading in concert. The room was packed as full of everybody's ma as it could be, and yet not mash the children out of shape, and a whole lot of young ones would read a piece together. Fine? Finest thing you ever heard. I remember one time teacher must have calculated a leetle mite too close, or else one girl more was in the class than she had reckoned on; but on the day, the two end girls just managed to stand upon the platform and that was all. They recited together:

"There was a sound of revelry by night
And Belgium's capital . . . . "

I forget the rest of it. Well, anyhow, they were supposed to make gestures all together. Teacher had rehearsed the gestures, and they all did it simultaneously, just as if they had been wound up with a spring. But, as I said, the two end girls had all they could do to keep on the platform, and it takes elbow room for: "'T is but the car rattling over the stony street," and one girl - well, she said she stepped off on purpose, but I didn't believe her then and I don't now. We had our laugh about it, whichever way it was.

We had our laugh . . . . Ah, life was all laughter then. That was before care came to be the shadow at our heel. That was before black Sorrow met us in the way, and would not let us pass unless we gave to her our dearest treasure. That was before we learned that what we covet most is, when we get it, but a poor thing after all, that whatsoever chalice Fortune presses to our lips, a tear is in the bottom of the cup. In those happy days gone by if the rain fell, 't was only for a little while, and presently the sky was bright again, and the birds whistled merrily among the wet and shining leaves. Now "the clouds return after the rain."

It can never be with us again as once it was. For us the bell upon the Old Red School-house calls in vain. We heed it not, we that hearkened for it years ago. The living tide of youth flows toward the school-house, and we are not of it. Never again shall we sit at those old desks, whittled and carved with rude initials, and snap our fingers, eager to tell the answer. Never again shall we experience the thrill of pride when teacher praised us openly. Never again shall we sit trembling while the principal, reads the note, and then scowls at us fiercely with: "Take off your coat, sir!" Ah, me! Never again, never again.

Well, who wants it to be that way again? We're men and women now. We've duties and responsibilities.

Who wants to be a child again? Not I. Let me stick just at my present age for about a hundred years, and I'll never utter a word of complaint.

Eugene Wood

THE SABBATH-SCHOOL

"We-a love the Sunday-school.
We-a love the Sunday-school.
(Girls) - So do I.
(Boys)-So do I.
(School) - We all love the Sunday-school."

SPARKLING DEWDROPS."

Some people believe that when General Conference assigned them to the Committee on Hymn-Book Revision, power and authority were given unto them to put a half-sole and a new heel on any and all poetry that might look to them to be a little run over on one side. If they felt as I do about the lines that head this article they would have "Sunday" scratched out and "Sabbath" written in before you could bat an eye. The mere substitution of one word for another may seem a light matter to a man that has never composed anything more literary than an obituary for the Western Advocate of Sister Jane Malinda Sprague, who was born in Westmoreland County, Pennsylvania, in 1816, removed with her parents at a tender age to New Sardis, Washington County, Ohio, where, etc., etc. If he wanted to extract a word he would do it, and never even offer to give the author gas. But I know just how it hurts. I know or can imagine how the gifted poet that penned the deathless lines I have quoted must have walked the floor in an agony until every word and syllable was just to suit him, and so, though I feel sure he meant to write "Sabbath-school," I don't dare change it.

To most persons one word seems about as good as another, Sunday or Sabbath, but when there are young people about the house you learn to be careful how you talk before them. Now, I would not go so far as to say that "Sunday" is what you might call exactly rowdy, but er . . . but . . . er . . . Let me illustrate. If a man says, "It's a beautiful Sunday morning," like enough he has on red-and-green stockings, baggy knickerbockers, a violet-and-purple sweater, a cap shaped like a milk-roll, and is smoking a pipe. He very likely carries a bagful of golf-sticks, or is pumping up his bicycle. But if a man says, "This beautiful Sabbath morn," you know for a certainty that he wears a long-tailed black coat, a boiled shirt, and a white tie. He is bald from his forehead upward, his upper lip is shaven, and his views and those of the late Robert Reed on the disgusting habit of using tobacco are absolutely at one.

Not alone a regard for respectability, but the hankering to be historically accurate, urges me to make the change I speak of. Originally the institution was a Sunday-school, and not very respectable either. I should hate to think any of my dear young friends were in the habit of attending such a low-class affair as Robert Raikes conducted. Sunday-schools were for "little ragamuffins," as he called them, who worked such long hours on week-days (from five in the morning until nine at night) that if they were to learn the common branches at all it had to be on a Sunday. A ragged school was bad enough in itself, putting foolish notions into the heads of gutter-brats and making them discontented and unhappy in their lot; but to teach a ragged school on Sunday was a little too much. So Robert Raikes encountered the most violent opposition, although from that beginning dates popular education in England.

To be able to read is no Longer a sign that Pa can afford to do without the young ones' wages on a Saturday night, and can even pay for their schooling. It is no longer a mark of wealth or even of hard-won privilege, but the common fate of all; to know the three R's, and Sunday is not now set apart for secular instruction. So good and wholesome an institution as the Sunday-school was not permitted to perish, but was changed to suit the environment. It is now become the Sabbath-school for the study of the Bible, a Christian recrudescence of the synagogue. For some eighteen centuries it was supposed that a regularly ordained minister should have exclusive charge of this work. At rare intervals nowadays a clergyman may be found to maintain that because a man has been to college and to the theological seminary, and has made the study of the Scriptures his life-work (moved to that decision after careful self-examination) that therefore he is better fitted to that ministry than Miss Susie Goldrick, who teaches a class in Sabbath-school very acceptably. Miss Goldrick is in the second year in the High School, and last Friday afternoon read a composition on English Literatoor, in which she spoke in terms of high praise of John Bunion, the well-known author of " Progress and Poverty." Miss Goldrick is very conscientious, and always keeps her thumbnail against the questions printed on the lesson-leaf, so as not to ask twice, "What did the disciples then do?"

It were a grave error to suppose that no secular learning is acquired in the modern Sabbath-school. I remember once, when quite young, speaking to my teacher, in the interval between the regular class work and the closing exercises, about peacocks. I had read of them, but had never seen one. What did they look like? She said a peacock was something like a butterfly. I have always remembered that, and when I did finally see a peacock, I was interested to note the essential accuracy of the description.

Also, one day a new lady taught our class, Miss Evans having gone up to Marion to spend a Sunday with her brother, who kept a stove store there, and this new lady borrowed two flower vases from off the pulpit and a piece of string from Turkey-egg McLaughlin to explain to us boys how the earth went around the sun. We had too much manners to tell her that we knew that years and years ago when we were in Miss Humphreys's room. I don't remember what the earth going around the sun had to do with the lesson for the day, which was about Samuel anointing David's head with oil - did I ever tell you how I anointed my own head with coal oil? - but I do remember that she broke both the vases and cut her finger, and had to keep sucking it the rest of the time, because she didn't want to get her handkerchief all bloodied up. It was a kind of fancy handkerchief, made of thin stuff trimmed with lace - no good.

The Sabbath-school may be said to be divided into three courses, namely, the preparatory or infant-class, the collegiate or Sabbath-school proper, and the post-graduate or Mr. Parker's Bible-class.

What can a mere babe of three or four years learn in

Sabbath-school? sneers the critic. Not much, I grant you, of justification by Faith, or Effectual Calling; but certain elementary precepts can be impressed upon the mind while it is still in a plastic condition that never can be wholly obliterated, come what may in after life. Prime among these elementary precepts is this: "Always bring a penny."

Some one has said, "Give me the first seven years of a child's life and I care not who has the remainder." I cannot endorse this without reserve; but I maintain as a demonstrated fact: "Bring up a child to contribute a copper cent, and when he is old he will not depart from it." It was recently my high privilege to attend a summer gathering of representative religious people in the largest auditorium in this country. Sometimes under that far-spreading roof ten thousand souls were assembled and met together. This fact could be guessed at with tolerable accuracy from the known seating capacity, but the interesting thing was that it could be predicated with mathematical certainty that exactly ten thousand people were present, because the offertory footed up exactly one hundred dollars. What an encouragement to these faithful infant-class teachers that have labored unremittingly, instant in season and out of season, saying over and over again with infinite patience, "Always bring a penny," to know that their labor has not been in vain, and that as a people we have made it the rule of our lives always to bring a penny - and no more.

I have often tried to think what a Sabbath-school must be like in California, where they have no pennies. It seems hardly possible that the institution can exist under such a patent disability, and yet it does. Do they work it on the same principle as the post-office in that far-off land where you 'cannot buy one postal card because the postmaster cannot make change, but must buy five postal cards or two two-cent stamps and a postal? In other words, does a nickel, the smallest extant coin, serve for five persons for one Sunday or one person for five Sundays? I have often wondered about this.

Subsidiary instruction in the preparatory course consists of sitting right still and being nice, keeping your fingers out of Johnny Pym's eye, because it hurts him and makes him cry, not grabbing in the basket when it goes by, even though it does have pennies in it, coaching in a repertory of songs like: "Beautiful, Beautiful Little Hands," "You in Your Little Corner and I in Mine," " The Consecrated Cross-Eyed Bear," "Pass Around the Wash-Rag" - the grown folks call that "Pass Along the Watchword" and stories about David and Goliath, Samson and the three hundred foxes with fire tied to their tails, Moses in the bulrushes, the infant Samuel, Hagar in the wilderness, and so forth. The clergy have often objected that these stories, being told at the same period of life with those about Santa Claus, "One time there was a little boy and he had a dog named Rover," the little girl that had hair as black as ebony, skin as white as snow, and cheeks as red as blood, because her Ma, who was a queen by occupation, happened to cut her finger with a black-handled knife along about New Year's - the clergy, I say, have often objected that all these matters, being brought to a child's attention at the same period in its life, are likely to be regarded in after years as of equal evidential value. I am not much of a hand to argue, myself, but I should like to have one of these carping critics meet my friend, Mrs. Sarah M. Boggs, who has taught the infant-class since 1867, having missed only two Sundays in that time, once, in 1879, when it stormed so that nobody in town was out, and once, last winter a year ago, when she slipped off the back porch and hurt her knee. I can just see Sister Boggs laying down the law to anybody that finds fault with the infant-class, let him be preacher or who. Why the very idea! Do you mean to say, sir - I guess Sister Boggs can straighten him out all right.

No less faithful is Mr. Parker, the leading lawyer of the town, who conducts the Bible-class. I believe one morning he didn't get there until after the last bell was done ringing, but otherwise his record of attendance compares favorably with Sister Boggs's. Both teachers agree to ignore the stated lesson for the day, but whereas Sister Boggs leads her flock through the flowery meads of narration, Mr. Parker and his class have camped out by preference for the last forty years in the arid wilderness of Romans and Hebrews and Corinthians First and Second, flinging the plentiful dornicks of "Paul says this" and "Paul says that" at each other's heads in friendly strife. Mr. Parker's class is also very assiduous in its attendance upon the Young People's meetings, seemingly holding the dogma, "Once a young person always a young person." The prevailing style of hairdressing among the members is to grow the locks long on the left side of the head, and to bring the thin layer across to the right, pasted down very carefully with a sort of peeled onion effect.

There is a whole lot of them, and they jower away at each other all through the time between the opening and the closing exercises, having the liveliest kind of a time getting over about two verses of the Bible and the whole ground of speculative theology.

Immeasurably more impermanent in method and personnel is the regular collegiate department, the Sabbath-school proper. In the early days, away back when sugar was sixteen cents a pound, the thing to do was to learn Scripture verses by heart. If you were a rude, rough boy who didn't exactly love the Sunday-school as much as the hymn made you say you did, but still one who had rather sing it than stir up a muss, you hunted for the shortest verses you could find and said them off. From four to eight was considered a full day's work. But if you were a boy who put on an apron and helped your Ma with the dishes, a boy who always wiped your feet before you came in, a boy that never got kept in at school, a boy that cried pretty easy, a nice, pale boy, with bulging blue eyes, you came to Sabbath-school and disgorged verses like buck-shot out of a bag. The four-to-eight-verse boys sat and listened, and improved their minds. There was generally one other boy like you in the class, and it was nip-and-tuck between you which should get the prize, until finally you came one Sunday, all bloated up with 238 verses in your craw, and he quit discouraged. The prize was yours. It was a beautiful little Bible with a brass clasp; it had two tiny silk strings of an old-gold color for bookmarks, and gilt edges all around that made the leaves stick together at first. It was printed in diamond type, so small it made your ears ring when you tried to read it.

Other faculties than that of memory were called into action in those days by problems like these: "Who was the meekest man? Who was the strongest man? Who was the father of Zebedee's children? Who had the iron bedstead, and whose thumbs and great-toes were cut off?" To set a child to find these things in the Bible without a concordance seems to us as futile as setting him to hunt a needle in a haystack. But our fathers were not so foolish as we like to think them; they didn't care two pins if we never discovered who had the iron bedstead, but they knew that, leafing over the book, we should light upon treasure where we sought it not, kernels of the sweetest meat in the hardest shells, stories of enthralling interest where we least expected them, but, most of all, and best of all, texts that long afterward in time of trouble should come to us, as it were the voice of one that also had eaten the bread of affliction, calling to us across the chasm of the centuries and saying: "O, tarry thou the Lord's leisure: be strong and He shall comfort thine heart."

In the higher classes, that still were not high enough to rank with Mr. Parker's, the exegetical powers were stimulated in this wise: "'And they sung a hymn and went out.' Now what do you understand by that?" We told what we "understood," and what we "held," and what we "believed," and laid traps for the teacher and tried to corner him with irrelevant texts wrenched from their context. He had to be an able man and a nimble-witted man. Mere piety might shine in the prayer-meeting, in the class-room, at the quarterly love-feast, but not in the Sabbath-school. I remember once when Brother Butler was away they set John Snyder to teach us. John didn't know any more than the law allowed, and we made him feel it, until finally, badgered beyond endurance, he blurted out that all he knew was that he was a sinner saved by grace. Maybe he couldn't just tell where to find this, that, and t' other thing in the Bible, but he could turn right to the place where it said that though a body's sins were as scarlet, yet they should be white as snow. It was regarded as a very poor sort of an excuse then, but thinking it over here lately , it has seemed to me that maybe John had the root of the matter in him after all.

The comparative scarcity of polemical athletes and the relative plenty of the Miss Susie Goldrick kind of teachers, apparently called into being the Berean Lesson Leaf system, with its Bible cut up into lady-bites of ten or twelve verses, its Golden Topics, Golden Texts, its apt alliterations, like:

S AMUEL
    EEKS
    AUL
    ORROWING

and its questions prepared in tabloid form, suitable for the most enfeebled digestions, see directions printed on inside wrapper. Among the many evidences of the degeneracy of the age is the scandalous ignorance of our young people regarding the sacred Scriptures, which at the very lowest estimate are incontestably the finest English ever written. Those whose childhood antedates the lesson leaf are not so unfamiliar with that wondrous treasure-house of thought. It is not for me to say what has wrought the change. I can only point out that lesson leaves, being about the right size for shaving papers, barely last from Sunday to Sunday, while that very identical Bible with the blinding type that I won years and years ago, by learning verses, is with me still. Yes, and as I often wonder to discover, some of those very verses that I gobbled down as heedlessly as any ostrich are with me still.

Remain to be considered the opening and closing exercises, principally devoted, I remember, to learning new tunes and singing old ones out of books with pretty titles, like "Golden Censer," "Silver Spray,"

"Pearl and Gold," "Sparkling Dewdrops," and "Sabbath Chimes." I wasn't going to tell it, but I might as well, I suppose. I can remember as far back as "Musical Leaves." There must be quite a lot of people scattered about the country who sung out of that when they were little. I wish a few of us old codgers might get together some time and with many a hummed and prefatory, "Do, mi, Sol, do; Sol, mi . . . mi-i-i-i," finally manage to quaver out the sweet old tunes we learned when we were little tads, each with a penny in his fat, warm hand: "Shall we Gather at the River?" and "Work, for the Night is Coming"; and what was the name of that one about:

"The waves shall come and the rolling thunder shock
 Shall beat upon the house that is founded on a rock,
 And it never shall fall, never, never, never."

What the proper English tune is to "I think when I read that sweet story of old" I cannot tell, but I am sure it can never melt my heart as that one in the old "Musical Leaves." with its twistful repetitions of the last line:

"I should like to have been with Him then,
 I should like to have been with Him then,
 When He took little children like lambs to His fold,
 I should like to have been with Him then."

I fear we could not sing that without breaking down. As we recall it, we draw an inward fluttering breath, something grips our throats and makes them ache, our eyes blur, and a tear slips down upon the cheek, not of sorrow - God knows not all of sorrow - but if we had it all to live over again, how differently we - oh, well, it's too late now, but still.

Leafing over my little girl's "Arabian Nights" the other day, when I came to the story of "The Enchanted Horse," I found myself humming, "Land ahead! Its fruits are waving." My father used to lead the singing in Sabbath-school, and when he was sol-fa-ing that tune to learn it, I was devouring that story, and was just about at the picture where Prince What's-his-name rises up into the air on the Enchanted Horse, with his true love hanging on behind, and all the multitude below holding their turbans on as they look up and exclaim: "Well, if that don't beat the Dutch!"

And another tune still excites in me the sullen resentment that it did when I first heard it. In those days, just as a fellow got to the exciting part in "Frank at Don Carlos's Ranch," or whatever the book was, there was kindling to be split, or an armful of wood to be brought in, or a pitcher of water from the well, or "run over to Mrs. Boggs's and ask her if she won't please lend me her fluting-iron," or "run down to Galbraith's and get me a spool of white thread, Number 60, and hurry right back, because then I want you to go over to Serepta Downey's and take her that polonaise pattern she asked me to cut out for her," or - there was always something on hand. So what should one of these composers do - I don't know what ever possessed the man - but go write a Sabbath-school song with this chorus:

> "There'll be something to do,
> There'll be something to do,
> There'll be something for children to do:
> On that bright shining shore,
> Where there's joy evermore,
> There'll be something for children to do."

Eugene Wood

I suppose he thought that would be an inducement!

One of these days America is going to be the musical center of the world. When that day is fully come, and men sit down to write about it, I hope they won't forget to give due credit to the reed organ, Stephen Foster, and the Sabbath-school. The reed organ had a lot to do with musical culture. It is much decried now by people that prefer a piano that hasn't been tuned for four years; but the reed organ will come into its own some day, don't forget. Without it the Sabbath-school could not have been. Anybody that would have a piano in a Sabbath-school ought to be prosecuted.

When music, heavenly maid, was just coming to after that awful lick the Puritans hit her, the first sign of returning life was that people began to tire of the ten or a dozen tunes to which our great-grandfathers droned and snuffled all their hymns. In those days there was raised up a man named Stephen Foster, who "heard in his soul the music of wonderful melodies," and we have been singing them ever since - "'Way Down upon the Swanee Ribber," and "Old Kentucky Home," and "Nellie Gray," and the rest. Then Bradbury and Philip Phillips and many more of them began to write exactly the same kind of tunes for sacred words. They were just the thing for the Sabbath-school, but they were more, much more.

You know that when a fellow gets so he can shave himself without cutting half his lip off, when it takes him half an hour to get the part in his hair to suit him, when he gets in the way of shining his shoes and has a pretty taste in neckties, he doesn't want to bawl the air of a piece like the old stick-in-the-muds up in the Amen corner or in Mr. Parker's class. He wants to sing bass. Air is too high for him anyhow unless he sings it with a hog noise. Oh, you get out! You do, too, know what a "hog noise" is. You want to let on you've always lived in town. Likely story if you never heard anybody in the hog-pasture with a basket of nubbins calling, "Peeg! Peeg! Boo-eel Booee!" A man's voice breaks into falsetto on the "Boo-ee!" Well, anyhow, such a young man as I am telling you of would be ashamed to sing with a hog noise. He wants to sing bass. Now the regular hymn-tunes change the bass as often as they change the soprano, and if you go fumbling about for the note, by the time you get it right it is wrong, because the tune has gone on and left you. The Sabbath-school songs had the young man Absalom distinctly in view. They made the bass the same all through the measure, and all the changes were strictly on the do, sol and fa basis. As far as the other notes in the scale were concerned, the young man Absalom need not bother his head with them. With do, sol and fa he could sing through the whole book from cover to cover as good as anybody.

When people find out what fun it is to sing by note, it is only a step to the "Messiah," two blocks up and turn to the right, as you might say. After that, it is only going ahead till you get to "Vogner." Yes, and many's the day you called the hogs. Don't tell me.

Once a month on Sunday evenings there were Sabbath-school concerts. The young ones sat in the front seats, ten or twelve in a pew. "Now, children," said the superintendent, "I want you all to sing loud and show the folks how nice you can sing. Page 65. Sixty-fi'th page, 'Scatter Seeds of Kindness.' Now, all sing out now." We licked our thumbs and scuffled through the book till we found the place. We scowled at it, and stuck out our mouths at it, and shrieked at it, and bawled at it, and did the very best we knew to give an imitation of two hundred little pigs all grabbed by the hind leg at once. That was what made folks call it a concert.

There were addresses to the dear children by persons that teetered on their toes and dimpled their cheeks in dried-apple smiles as us. Some complain that they do not know how to talk to children and keep them interested. Oh, pshaw! Simple as A B C. Once you learn the trick you can talk to the little folks for an hour and a half on "Banking as Related to National Finance," and keep them on the quiver of excitement. Ask questions. And to be sure that they give the right answers (a very important thing) remember this: When you wish them to say "Yes, sir," end your question with "Don't they?" or "isn't it?" When you wish them to say "No, sir," end your question with "Do they?" or "Is it?" When you wish them to choose between two answers, mention first the one they mustn't take, then pause, look archly at them, and mention the one they must take. Thus:

Q. - Now, dear children, I wonder if you can tell me where the sun rises. In the north, doesn't it ?

A. - Yes, sir.

Q. - Yes, you are right. In the north. And because it rises in the north every afternoon at three, how do we walk about? On our feet, do we?

A. - No, sir.

Q. - No. Of course not. Then how is it we do walk

about ? On our ears or - (now the look) on our noses?

A. - On our noses.

This method, if carefully and systematically employed, was never known to fail. It is called the Socratic method.

The most interesting feature of the monthly Sabbath-school concert is universally conceded to be the treasurer's report. So much on hand at the last meeting, so much contributed by each class during the month last past, so much expended, so much left on hand at present. We used to sit and listen to it with slack jaws and staring eyes. Money, money, oceans of money! Thirty-eight cents and seventy-six cents and a dollar four cents! My!

The librarian's report was nowhere. It was a bully library, too, and contained the "Through by Daylight" Series, and the "Ragged Dick" Series, and the "Tattered Tom" Series, and the "Frank on the Gunboat" Series, and the "Frank the Young Naturalist" Series, and the "Elm Island" Series - Did you ever read "The Ark of Elm Island", and "Giant Ben of Elm Island"? You didn't? Ah, you missed it - and the "B. O. W. C." Series - and say! there was a book in that library - oo-oo! "Cast up by the Sea," all about wreckers, and false lights on the shore, and adventures in Central Africa, and there's a nigger queen that wants to marry him, and he don't want to because he loves a girl in England - I think that's kind of soft - and he kills about a million of them trying to get away. You want to get that book. Don't let them give you "Patient Henry" or "Charlie Watson, the Drunkard's Little Son."

They're about boys that take sick and die - no good.

It was a bully library, but the report wasn't interesting. Major Humphreys's always was. He was the treasurer because he worked in the bank. He came from the Western Reserve, and said "cut" when he meant coat, and "hahnt" when he meant heart. I can shut my eyes and hear him read his report now: "Infant-class, Mrs. Sarah M. Boggs, one dolla thutty-eight cents; Miss Dan'ells's class, fawty-six cents; Miss Goldrick's class, twenty-faw cents; Mr. Pahnker's class, ninety-three cents; Miss Rut's class, naw repawt."

Poor old Miss Root! There was hardly ever any report from her class. Often she hadn't a penny to give, and perhaps the other old ladies, who found the keenest possible delight in doing what they called "running up the references," had no more, for they were relics of an age when women weren't supposed to have money to fling right and left in the foolish way that women will if they're not looked after - shoes for the baby, and a new calico dress every two or three years or so.

Yes, it is rather interesting for a change now and then to hear these folks go on about what a terrible thing the Sabbath-school is, and how it does more harm than good. They get really excited about it, and storm around as if they expected folks to take them seriously. They know, just as well as we do, that this wouldn't be any kind of a country at all if we couldn't look back and remember the Sabbath-school, or if we couldn't fix up the children Sunday afternoons, and find their lesson leaves for them, and hunt up a penny to give to the poor heathen, and hear them say the Golden Text before they go, and tell them to be nice. Papa and mamma watch them from the window till they turn the corner, and then go back to the Sunday paper with a secure sort of feeling. They won't learn anything they oughtn't to at the Sabbath-school.

THE REVOLVING YEAR

"'It snows!' cries the schoolboy, 'Hurrah!'
And his shout is heard through parlor and hall."

MCGUFFEY's THIRD READER.

(Well, maybe it was the Second Reader. And if it was the Fourth, what difference does it make? And, furthermore, who 's doing this thing, you or me?)

Had it not been that never in my life have I ever heard anybody say either "It snows!" or "Hurrah!" it is improbable that I should have remembered the first line of a poem describing the effect produced upon different kinds of people by the sight of the first snowstorm of winter. Had it not been for the plucky (not to say heroic) effort to rhyme "hall" with "hurrah" I should not have remembered the second, and still another line of it, depicting the emotions of a poor widow with a large family and a small woodpile, is burned into my memory only by reason of the shocking language it contains, the more shocking in that it was deliberately put forth to be read by innocent-minded children. Poor Carrie Rinehart! When she stood up to read that, she got as red as a beet, and I believed her when she told me afterward that she thought she would sink right through that floor. Of course, some had to snicker, but the most of us, I am thankful to say, were a credit to our bringing up, and never let on we heard it. All the same it was a terrible thing to have to speak right out loud before everybody. If any of the boys (let alone the girls), had said that because he felt like saying it, he would have been sent in to the principal, and that night his daddy would have given him another licking.

Even now I cannot bring myself to write the line without toning it down.

"'It snows!' cries the widow. 'Oh G - d!'"

At the beginning of winter, I will not deny, that the schoolboy might have shouted: "It's snowin'! Hooee!" when he saw the first snow flakes sifting down, and realized that the Old Woman was picking her geese. A change is always exciting, and winter brings many joyous sports and pastimes, skating, and snowballing, and sliding down hill, and - er - er - I said skating didn't I? and - er - Oh, yes, sleigh-riding, and - er - Well, I guess that's about all.

Skating, now, that's fine. I know a boy who, when the red ball goes up in the street-cars, sneaks under his coat a pair of wooden-soled skates, with runners that curl up over the toes like the stems of capital letters in the Spencerian copy-book. He is ashamed of the old-fashioned things, which went out of date long and long before my day, but he says that they are better than the hockeys. Well, you take a pair of such skates and strap them on tightly until you can't tell by the feel which is feet and which is wooden soles, and you glide out upon the ice above the dam for, say about four hours, with the wind from the northwest and the temperature about nine below, and I tell you it is something grand. And if you run over a stick that is frozen in the ice, or somebody bumps into you, or your feet slide out from under you, and you strike on your ear and part of your face on the ice, and go about ten feet ah, it's great! Simply great. And it's nice too, to skate into an air-hole into water about up to your neck, and have the whole mob around you whooping and "hollering" and slapping their legs with glee, because they know it isn't deep enough to drown you, and you look so comical trying to claw out. And when you do get out, it takes such along time to get your skates of, and you feel so kind of chilly like, and when you get home your clothes are frozen stiff on you - Oh, who would willingly miss such sport?

And sleigh-riding! Me for sleigh-riding! You take a nice, sharp day in winter, when the sky is as blue as can be because all the moisture is frozen out of the air, a day when the snow under the sleigh runners whines and creaks, as if thousands of tiny wineglasses were being crushed by them, and the bells go jing-jing, jing-jing on the frosty air which just about takes the hide off your face; when you hold your mittens up to your ears and then have to take them down to slap yourself across the chest to get the blood agoing in your fingers; when you kick your feet together and dumbly wonder why it is your toes don't click like marbles; when the cold creeps up under your knitted pulse-warmers, and in at every possible little leak until it has soaked into your very bones; when you snuggle down under the lap-robe where it is warm as toast (day before yesterday's toast) and try to pull your shoulders up over your head; when a little drop hangs on the end of your nose, which has ceased to feel like a living, human nose, and now resembles something whittled to a point; when you hold your breath as long as you can, and your jaw waggles as if you were playing chin-chopper with it - Ah, that's the sport of kings! And after you have got as cold as you possibly can get, and simply cannot stand it a minute longer, you ride and ride and ride and ride and ride and ride and ride and ride and ride. Once in a while you turn out for another sleigh, and nearly upset in the process, and you can see that in all points its occupants are exactly as you are, just as happy and contented. There aren't any dogs to run out and bark at you. Old Maje and Tige, and even little Bounce and Guess are snoozing behind the kitchen stove. All there is is just jing-jing, jing-jing, jing-jing, not a bird-cry or a sound of living creature. jing-jing, jing-jing. . . . . Well, yes, kind o' monotonous, but still . . . . You pass a house, and a woman comes out to scrape off a plate to the chickens standing on one foot in a corner where the sun can get at them, and the wind cannot. She scrapes slowly, and looks at you as much as to say: "I wonder who's sick. Must be somebody going for the doctor, day like this." And then she shudders: "B-b-b-oo-oo-oo!" and runs back into the house and slams the door hard. You snuffle and look at the chimney that has thick white smoke coming out of it, and consider that very likely a nice, warm fire is making all that smoke, and you snuffle again, and ride and ride and ride and ride and ride and ride and ride and 'ride. And about an hour and a half after you have given up all hopes, and are getting resigned to your fate, you turn off the big road and up the lane to the house where you are going on your pleasure-trip, and you hop out as nimble as a sack of potatoes, and hobble into the house, and don't say how-de-do or anything, but just make right for the stove. The people all squall out: "Why, ain't you 'most froze?" and if you answer, "Yes sum," it's as much as ever. Generally you can't do anything but just stand and snuffle and look as if you hadn't a friend on earth. And about the time you get so that some spots are pretty warm, and other spots aren't as cold as they were, why then you wrap up, and go home again with the same experience, only more so. Fine! fine!

It's nice, too, when there's a whole crowd out together in a wagon-bed with straw in it. There's something so cozy in straw! And the tin horns you blow in each other's ear, and the songs you sing: "Jingle bells, jingle bells, jingle all the way," and "Waw-unneeta! Waw-unneeta, ay-usk thy sowl if we shud part," and "Nearer, my God, to Thee," and "Johnny Shmoker," and that variation of "John Brown's Body," where every time you sing over the verse you leave off one more word, and somebody always forgets, and you laugh fit to kill yourself, and just have a grand time. And maybe you take a whole lot of canned cove oysters with you, and when you get out to Makemson's, or wherever it is you're going, Mrs. Makemson puts the kettle on and makes a stew, cooking the oysters till they are thoroughly done. And she makes coffee, the kind you can't tell from tea by the looks, and have to try twice before you can tell by the taste. Ah! winter brings many joyous sports and pastimes. And you get back home along about half-past two, and the fire's out, and the folks are in bed, and you have to be at the store to open up at seven - Laws! I wish it was so I could go sleigh-riding once more in the long winter evenings, when the pitcher in the spare bedroom bursts, and makes a noise like a cannon.

And sliding down hill, I like that.

What? Coasting? Never heard of it. If it's anything like

sliding down hill, it's all right. For a joke you can take a barrel-stave and hold on to that and slide down. It goes like a scared rabbit, but that isn't so much the point as that it slews around and spills you into a drift. Sleds are lower and narrower than they used to be, and they also lack the artistic adornment of a pink, or a blue, or a black horse, painted with the same stencil but in different colors, and named "Dexter," or "Rarus," or"Goldsmith Maid." These are good names, but nobody ever called his sled by a name. Boggs's hill, back of the lady's house that taught the infant-class in Sunday-school, was a good hill. It had a creek at the bottom, and a fine, long ride, eight or ten feet, on the ice. But Dangler's hill was the boss. It was the one we all made up our minds we would ride down some day when the snow was just right. We'd go over there' and look up to the brow of the hill and say: "Gee! But wouldn't a fellow come down like sixty, though?"

"Betchy!"

We'd look up again, and somebody would say: "Aw, come on. Less go over to Boggs's hill."

"Thought you was goin' down Dangler's."

"Yes, I know, but all the other fellows is over to Boggs's."

"A-ah, ye're afraid."

"Ain't either."

"Y' are teether."

"I dare you."

"Oh, well now - "

"I double dare you."

"All right. I will if you will. You go first."

"Nah, you go first. The fellow that's dared has got to go first. Ain't that so, Chuck? Ain't that so, Monkey?"

"I'll go down if you will, on'y you gotta go first."

"Er - er - Who all 's over at Boggs's hill?"

"Oh, the whole crowd of 'em, Turkey-egg McLaughlin, and Ducky Harshberger, and - Oh, I don' know who all."

"Tell you what less do. Less wait till it gets all covered with ice, and all slick and smooth. Then less come over and go down."

"Say, won't she go like sixty then! Jeemses Rivers! Come on, I'll beat you to the corner."

That was the closest we ever came to going down Dangler's hill. Railroad hill wasn't so bad, over there by the soap-factory, because they didn't run trains all the time, and you stood a good chance of missing being run over by the engine, but Dangler's Well, now, I want to tell you Dangler's was an awful steep hill, and a long one, and when you think that it was so steep nobody ever pretended to drive up it even in the summer-time, and you slide down the hill and think that, once you got to going.

Fun's fun , I know, but nobody wants to go home with

half his scalp hanging over one eye, and dripping all over the back porch. Because, you know, a fellow's mother gets crosser about blood on wood-work than anything else. Scrubbing doesn't do the least bit of good; it has to be planed off, or else painted.

Let me see, now. Have I missed anything? I'll count 'em off on my fingers. There's skating, and sleigh-riding, and sliding down hill, and Oh, yes. Snowballing and making snow-men. Nobody makes a snow-man but once, and nobody makes a snow-house after it has caved in on him once and like to killed him. And as for snowballing - Look here. Do you know what's the nicest thing about winter? Get your feet on a hot stove, and have the lamp over your left shoulder, and a pan of apples, and something exciting to read, like "Frank Among the Indians." Eh, how about it? In other words, the best thing about winter is when you can forget that it is winter.

The excitement that prompts "It snows!" and "Hurrah!" mighty soon peters out, and along about the latter part of February, when you go to the window and see that it is snowing again - again? Consarn the luck! - you and the poor widow with the large family and the small woodpile are absolutely at one.

You do get so sick and tired of winter. School lets out at four o'clock, and it's almost dark then. There's no time for play, for there's all that wood and kindling to get in, and Pap's awful cranky when he hops out of bed these frosty mornings to light the fire, and finds you've been skimpy with the kindling. And the pump freezes up, and you've got to shovel snow off the walks and out in the back-yard so Tilly can hang up the clothes when she comes to do the washing. And your mother is just as particular about your neck being clean as she is in summer when the water doesn't make you feel so shivery. And there's the bottle of goose-grease always handy, and the red flannel to pin around your throat, and your feet in the bucket of hot water before you go to bed - Aw, put 'em right in. Yes, I know it's hot. That's what going to make you well. In with 'em. Aw, child, it isn't going to scald you. Go on now. The water'll be stone-cold in a minute." Oh, I don't like winter for a cent. Kitchoo! There, I've gone and caught fresh cold.

I wish it would hurry up and come spring.

> "When the days begin to lengthen,
> The cold begins to strengthen."

Now, you know that doesn't stand to reason. Every day the sun inches a little higher in the heavens. His rays strike us more directly and for a longer time each day. But it's the cantankerous fact, and it simply has to stand to reason. That's the answer, and the sum has to be figured out somehow in accordance with it. Like one time, when I was about sixteen years old, and in the possession of positive and definite information about the way the earth went around the sun and all, I was arguing with one of these old codgers that think they know it all, one of these men that think it is so smart to tell you: "Sonny, when you get older, you'll know more 'n you do now - I hope. "Well, he was trying to tell me that the day lengthened at one end before it did at the other. I did my best to dispel the foolish notion from his mind, and explained to him how it simply could not be, but no, sir! he stood me down. Finally, since pure reasoning was wasted on him, I took the almanac off the nail it hung by, and - I bedog my riggin's if the old skidama link wasn't right after all. Sundown keeps coming a minute later every day, while, for quite a while there, sun-up sticks at the same old time, 7:3o A.M. Did you ever hear of anything so foolish?

"Very early, while it is yet dark," the alarm clock of old Dame Nature begins to buzz. It may snow and blow, and winter may seem to have settled in in earnest, but deep down in the earth, the root-tips, where lie the brains of vegetables, are gaping and stretching, and ho-humming, and wishing they could snooze a little longer. When it thaws in the afternoon and freezes up at sunset as tight as bricks, they tell me that out in the sugar-camp there are great doings. I don't know about it myself, but I have heard tell of boring a hole in the maple-tree, and sticking in a spout, and setting a bucket to catch the, drip, and collecting the sap, and boiling down, and sugaring off. I have heard tell of taffy-pullings, and how Joe Hendricks stuck a whole gob of maple-wax in Sally Miller's hair, and how she got even with him by rubbing his face with soot. It is only hearsay with me, but I'll tell you what I have done: I have eaten real maple sugar, and nearly pulled out every tooth I had in my head with maple-wax, and I have even gone so far as to have maple syrup on pancakes. It's good, too. The maple syrup came on the table in a sort of a glass flagon with a metal lid to it, and it was considered the height of bad manners to lick off the last drop of syrup that hung on the nose of the flagon. And yet it must not be allowed to drip on the table-cloth. It is a pity we can't get any more maple syrup nowadays, but I don't feel so bad about the loss of it, as I do to think what awful liars people can be, declaring on the label that 'deed and double, 'pon their word and honor, it is pure, genuine, unadulterated maple syrup, when they know just as well as they know anything that it is only store-sugar boiled up with maple chips.

Along about the same time, the boys come home with a ring of mud around their mouths, and exhaling spicy breaths like those which blow o'er Ceylon's isle in the hymn-book. They bear a bundle of roots, whose thick, pink hide mother whittles off with the butcher-knife and sets to steep. Put away the store tea and coffee. To-night as we drink the reddish aromatic brew we return, not only to our own young days, but to the young days of the nation when our folks moved to the West in a covered wagon; when grandpap, only a little boy then, about as big as Charley there, got down the rifle and killed the bear that had climbed into the hog-pen; when they found old Cherry out in the timber with her calf between her legs, and two wolves lying where she had horned them to death - we return to-night to the high, heroic days of old, when our forefathers conquered the wilderness and our foremothers reared the families that peopled it. This cup of sassafras to-night in their loving memory! Earth, rest easy on their moldering bones!

Some there be that still take stock in the groundhog. I don't believe he knows anything about it. And I believe that any animal that had the sense that he is reputed to have would not have remained a mere ground-hog all these years. At least not in this country. Anyhow, it's a long ways ahead, six weeks is, especially at the time when you do wish so fervently that it would come spring. We keep on shoveling coal in the furnace, and carrying out ashes, and longing and crying: "Oh, for pity's sakes! When is this going to stop?" And then, one morning, we awaken with a start Wha - what? Sh! Keep still, can't you? There is a more canorous and horn-like quality to the crowing of Gildersleeve's rooster, and his hens chant cheerily as they kick the litter about. But it wasn't these cheerful sounds that wakened us with a start. There! Hear that? Hear it? Two or three long-drawn, reedy notes, and an awkward boggle at a trill, but oh, how sweet! How sweet! It is the song-sparrow, blessed bird! It won't be long now; it won't be long.

The snow fort in the back-yard still sulks there black and dirty. "I'll go when I get good and ready, and not before," it seems to say. Other places the thinner snow has departed and left behind it mud that seizes upon your overshoe with an "Oh, what's your rush?" In the middle of the road it lies as smooth as pancake-batter. A load of building stone stalls, and people gather on the sidewalk to tell the teamster quietly and unostentatiously that he ought to have had more sense than to pile it on like that with the roads the way they are. Every time the cruel whip comes down and the horses dance under it, the women peering out of the front windows wince, and cluck "Tchk! Ain't it terrible? He ought to be arrested." This way and that the team turns and tugs, but all in vain. Somebody puts on his rubber boots and wades out to help, fearing not the muddy spokes. Yo hee! Yo hee! No use. He talks it over with the teamster. You can hear him say: "Well, suit yourself. If you want to stay here all night."

And then the women exult: "Goody! Goody! Serves him right. Now he has to take off some of the stone. Lazy man's load!"

The mother of children flies to the back-door when school lets out. "Don't you come in here with all that mud!" she squalls excitedly. "Look at you! A peck o' dirt on each foot. Right in my nice clean kitchen that I just scrubbed. Go 'long now and clean your shoes. Go 'long, I tell you. Slave and slave for you and that's all the thanks I get. You'd keep the place looking like a hogpen, if I wasn't at you all the time. I never saw such young ones since the day I was made. Never. Whoopin' and hollerin' and trackin' in and out. It's enough to drive a body crazy."

(Don't you care. It's just her talk. If it isn't one thing it's another, cleaning your shoes, or combing your hair, or brushing your clothes, or using your handkerchief, or shutting the door softly, or holding your spoon with your fingers and not in your fist, or keeping your finger out of your glass when you drink - something the whole blessed time. Forever and eternally picking at a fellow about something. And saying the same thing over and over so many times. That's the worst of it!)

Pap and mother read over the seed catalogues, all about "warm, light soils," and "hardy annuals," and "sow in drills four inches apart." It kind of hurries things along when you do that. In the south window of the kitchen is a box full of black dirt in which will you look out what you're doing? Little more and you'd have upset it. There are tomato seeds in that, I'll have you know. Oh, yes, government seeds. Somebody sends 'em, I don't know who. Congressman, I guess, whoever he is. I don't pretend to keep track of 'em. And say. When was this watered last? There it is. Unless I stand over you every minute - My land! If there's anything done about this house I've got to do it.

Between the days when it can't make up its mind whether to snow or to rain, and tries to do both at once, comes a day when it is warm enough (almost) to go without an overcoat. The Sunday following you can hardly hear what the preacher has to say for the whooping and barking. The choir members have cough drops in their cheeks when they stand up to sing, and everybody stops in at the drug store with: "Say, Doc, what's good for a cold?"

Eggs have come down. Yesterday they were nine for a quarter; to-day they're ten. Gildersleeve wants a dollar for a setting of eggs, but he'll let you have the same number of eggs for thirty cents if you'll wait till he can run a needle into each one. So afraid you'll raise chickens of your own.

Excited groups gather about rude circles scratched in the mud, and there is talk of "pureys," and "reals," and "aggies," and "commies," and "fen dubs!" There is a rich click about the bulging pockets of the boys, and every so often in school time something drops on the floor and rolls noisily across the room. When Miss Daniels asks: "Who did that?" the boys all look so astonished. Who did what, pray tell? And when she picks up a marble and inquires: "Whose is this?" nobody can possibly imagine whose it might be, least of all the boy whose most highly-prized shooter it is. At this season of the year, too, there is much serious talk as to the exceeding sinfulness of "playing for keeps." The little boys, in whose thumbs lingers the weakness of the arboreal ape, their ancestor, and who "poke" their marbles, drink in eagerly the doctrine that when you win a marble you ought to give it back, but the hard-eyed fellows, who can plunk it every time, sit there and let it go in one ear and out the other, there being a hole drilled through expressly for the purpose. What? Give up the rewards of skill? Ah, g'wan!

The girls, even to those who have begun to turn their hair up under, are turning the rope and dismally chanting: "All in together, pigs in the meadow, nineteen twenty, leave the rope empty," or whatever the rune is.

It won't be long now. It won't be long.

> "For lo; the winter is past, the rain is over and gone; the flowers appear on the earth; the time of the singing of birds is come, and the voice of the turtle is heard in our land; the fig-tree putteth forth her green figs, and the vines, with the tender grape give a good smell. Arise my love, my fair one and come away."

THE SONG OF SOLOMON.

Out in the woods the leaves that rustled so bravely when we shuffled our feet through them last fall are sodden and matted. It is warm in the woods, for the sun strikes down through the bare branches, and the cold wind is fended off. The fleshy lances of the spring beauty have stabbed upward through the mulch, and a tiny cup, delicately veined with pink, hangs its head bashfully. Anemones on brown wire stems aspire without a leaf, and in moist patches are May pinks, the trailing arbutus of the grown-ups. As we carry home a bunch, the heads all lopping every way like the heads of strangled babies, we can almost hear behind us in the echoing forests a long, heart-broken moan, as of Rachel mourning for her children, and will not be comforted because they are not. The wild flowers don't look so pretty in the tin cups of water as they did back in the woods. There is something cheap and common about them. Throw 'em out. The poor plants that planned through all the ages how to attract the first smart insects of the season, and trick them into setting the seeds for next years' flowers did not reckon that these very means whereby they hoped to rear a family would prove their undoing at the hands of those who plume themselves a little on their refinement, they "are so fond of flowers."

Old Winter hates to give up that he is beaten. It's a funny thing, but when you hear a person sing, "Good-a-by, Summer, good-a-by, good-a-by," you always feel kind of sad and sorry. It's going, the time of year when you can stay out of doors most of the time, when you can go in swimming, and the Sunday-school picnic, and the circus, and play base-ball and camp out, and there's no school, and everything nice, and watermelons, and all like that. Good-by, good-by, and you begin to sniff a little. The departure of summer is dignified and even splendid, but the earth looks so sordid and draggle-trailed when winter goes, that onions could not bring a tear. Old winter likes to tease. Aha! You thought I was gone, did you? Not yet, my child, not yet!" And he sends us huckleberry-colored clouds from the northwest, from which snow-flakes big as copper cents solemnly waggle down, as if they really expected the schoolboy to shout: "It snows! Hurrah!" and makes his shout heard through parlor and hall. But they only leave a few dark freckles on the garden beds. Alas, yes! There is no light without its shadow, no joy without its sorrow tagging after. It isn't all marbles and play in the gladsome springtide. Bub has not only to spade up the garden - there is some sense in that - but he has to dig up the flower beds, and help his mother set out her footy, trifling plants.

The robins have come back, our robins that nest each

spring in the old seek-no-further. To the boy grunting over the spading-fork presents himself Cock Robin. "How about it? Hey? All right? Hey?" he seems to ask, cocking his head, and flipping out the curt inquiries with tail-jerks. Glad of any excuse to stop work, the boy stands statue-still, while Mr. Robin drags from the upturned clods the long, elastic fish-worms, and then with a brief "Chip!" flashes out of sight. Be right still now. Don't move. Here he comes again, and his wife with him. They fly down, he all eager and alert to wait upon her, she whining and scolding. She doesn't think it's much of a place for worms. And there's that boy yonder. He's up to some devilment or other, she just knows. She oughtn't to have come away and left those eggs. They'll get cold now, she just knows they will. Anything might happen to them when she 's away, and then he 'll be to blame, for he coaxed her. He knows she told him she didn't want to come. But he would have it. For half a cent she'd go back right now. And, Heavens above! Is he going to be all 'day picking up a few little worms?

She cannot finish her sentences for her gulps, for he is tamping down in her insides the reluctant angleworms that do not want to die, two or three writhing in his bill at once, until he looks like Jove's eagle with its mouth full of thunderbolts. And all the time he is chip-chipping and flirting his tail, and saying: "How's that? All right? Hey? Here's another. How's that? All right? Hey? Open now. Like that? Here's one.

Oh, a beaut! Here's two fat ones? Great? Hey? Here y' go. Touch the spot? Hey? More? Sure Mike. Lots of 'em. Wide now. Boss. Hey? Wait a second - yes, honey. In a second. . . . I got him. Here's the kind you like. Oh, yes, do. Do take one more. Oh, you better."

"D' ye think I'm made o' rubber?" she snaps at him. "I know I'll have indigestion, and you'll be to bla - Mercy land! Them eggs!" and she gathers up her skirts and flits. He escorts her gallantly, but returns to pick a few for himself, and to cock his head knowingly at the boy, as much as to say: "Man of family, by Ned. Or - or soon will be. Oh, yes, any minute now, any minute."

And if I remember rightly, he even winks at the boy with a wink whose full significance the boy does not learn till many years after when it dawns upon him that it meant: "You got to make allowances for 'em. Especially at such a time. All upset, you know, and worried. Oh, yes. You got to; you got to make allowances for 'em."

Day by day the air grows balmier and softer on the cheek. Out in the garden, ranks of yellow-green pikes stand stiffly at "Present. Hump!" and rosettes of the same color crumple through the warm soil, unconsciously preparing for a soul tragedy. For an evening will come when a covered dish will be upon the supper-table, and when the cover is taken off, a subtle fragrance will betray, if the sense of sight do not, that the chopped-up lettuces and onions are in a marsh of cider vinegar, demanding to be eaten. And your big sister will squall out in comic distress: "Oh, ma! You are too mean for anything! Why did you have 'em tonight? I told you Mr. Dellabaugh was going to call, and you know how I love spring onions! Well, I don't care. I'm just going to, anyhow."

Things come with such a rush now, it is hard to tell what happens in its proper order. The apple-trees blossom out like pop-corn over the hot coals. The Japan quince repeats its farfamed imitation of the

Burning Bush of Moses; the flowering currants are strung with knobs of vivid yellow fringe; the dead grass from the front yard, the sticks and stalks and old tomato vines, the bits of rag and the old bones that Guess has gnawed upon are burning in the alley, and the tormented smoke is darting this way and that, trying to get out from under the wind that seeks to flatten it to the ground. All this is spring, and - and yet it isn't. The word is not yet spoken that sets us free to live the outdoor life; we are yet prisoners and captives of the house.

But, one day in school, the heat that yesterday was nice and cozy becomes too dry and baking for endurance. The young ones come in from recess red, not with the brilliant glow of winter, but a sort of scalded red. They juke their heads forward to escape their collars' moist embrace; they reach their hands back of them to pull their clinging winter underwear away. They fan themselves with joggerfies, and puff out: "Phew!" and look pleadingly at the shut windows. One boy, bolder than his fellows, moans with a suffering lament: "Miss Daniels, cain't we have the windows open? It's awful hot!" Frightful dangers lurk in draughts. Fresh air will kill folks. So, not until the afternoon is the prayer answered. Then the outer world, so long excluded, enters once more the school-room life. The mellifluous crowing of distant roosters, the rhythmic creaking of a thirsty pump, the rumble of a loaded wagon, the clinking of hammers at the blacksmith shop, the whistle of No. 3 away below town, all blend together in the soft spring air into one lulling harmony.

Winter's alert activity is gone. Who cares for grades and standings now? The girls, that always are so smart, gape lazily, and stare at vacancy wishing . . . . They don't know what they wish, but if He had a lot of money, why, then they could help the poor, and all like that, and have a new dress every day.

James Sackett - his real name is Jim Bag, but teacher calls him James Sackett - has his face set toward: "A farmer sold 16 2-3 bu. wheat for 66 7-8 c. per bu.; 19 2-9 bu. oats for," etc., etc., but his soul is far away in Cummins's woods, where there is a robbers' cave that he, and Chuck Higgins, and Bunt Rogers, and Turkey-egg McLaughlin are going to dig Saturday afternoons when the chores are done. They are going to - Here Miss Daniels should slip up behind him and snap his ear, but she, too, is far away in spirit. Her beau is coming after supper to take her buggy-riding. She wonders. . . . She wonders. . . . Will she have to teach again next fall? She wonders. . . .

Wait. Wait but a moment. A subtle change is coming.

The rim of the revolving year has a brighter and a darker half, a joyous and a somber half, Autumnal splendors cannot cheer the melancholy that we feel when summer goes from us, but when summer comes again the heart leaps up in glee to meet it. Wait but a moment now. Wait.

The distant woodland swims in an amethystine haze. A long and fluting note, honey-sweet as it were blown upon a bottle, comes to us from far. It is the turtle-dove. The blood beats in our ears. Arise, my love, my fair one, and come away.

So gentle it can scarce be felt, a waft of air blows over us, the first sweet breath of summer. A veil of faint and subtle perfume drifts around us. The vines with the tender grape give a good smell. And evermore as its enchantment is cast about us we are as once we were when first we came beneath its spell; we are by the smokehouse at the old home place; we stand in shoes whose copper toes wink and glitter in the sunlight, a gingham apron sways in the soft breeze, and on the green, upspringing turf dances the shadow of a tasseled cap. Life was all before us then. Please God, it is not all behind us now. Please God, our best and wisest days are yet to come the days when we shall do the work that is worthy of us. Dear one, mother of my children here and Yonder - and Yonder - the best and wisest days are yet to come. Arise, my love, my fair one, and come away.

THE SWIMMING-HOLE

It is agreed by all, I think, that the two happiest periods in a man's life are his boyhood and about ten years from now. We are exactly in the position described in the hymn:

> "Lo! On a narrow neck of land
> 'Twixt two unbounded seas we stand,
> And cast a wishful eye."

[I am told, on good authority, that this last line of the three belongs to another hymn. As it is just what I want to say, I'm going to let it stand as it is.]

If I remember right, the hymn went to the tune of "Ariel," and I can see John Snodgrass, the precentor, sneaking a furtive C from his pitch-pipe, finding E flat and then sol, and standing up to lead the singing, paddling the air gently with: Down, left, sing. Well, no matter about that now. What I am trying to get at, is that we have all a lost Eden in the past and a Paradise Regained in the future. 'Twixt two unbounded seas of happiness we stand on the narrow and arid sand-spit of the present and cast a wishful eye. In hot weather particularly the wishful eye, when directed toward the lost Eden of boyhood, lights on and lingers near the Old Swimming-hole.

Eugene Wood

I suppose boys do grow up into a reasonable enjoyment of their faculties in big seaside cities and on inland farms where there is no accessible body of water larger than a wash-tub, but I prefer to believe that the majority of our adult male population in youth went in swimming in the river up above the dam, where the big sycamore spread out its roots a-purpose for them to climb out on without muddying their feet. Some, I suppose, went in at the Copperas Banks below town, where the current had dug a hole that was "over head and hands," but that was pretty far and almost too handy for the boys from across the tracks.

The wash-tub fellows will have to be left out of it entirely. It was an inferior, low-grade Eden they had anyhow, and if they lost it, why, they 're not out very much that I can see. And I rather pity the boys that lived by the sea. They had a good time in their way, I suppose, with sailboats and things, but the ocean is a poor excuse for a swimming-hole. They say salt-water is easier to swim in; kind of bears you up more. Maybe so, but I never could see it; and even so, if it does, that slight advantage is more than made up for by the manifold disadvantages entailed. First place, there's the tide to figure on. If it was high tide last Wednesday at half-past ten in the morning, what time will it be high tide today? A boy can't always go when he wants to, and it is no fun to trudge away down to the beach only to find half a mile of soft, gawmy mud between him and the water. And he can't go in wherever it is deep enough and nobody lives near. People own the beach away out under water, and where he is allowed to go in may be a perfect submarine jungle of eel-grass or bottomed with millions of razor-edged barnacles that rip the soles of his feet into bleeding rags. Then, too, when one swims, more or less water gets into one's nose and mouth. River-water may not be exactly what a fastidious person would choose to drink habitually, but there is this in its favor as compared with sea-water: it will stay down after it is swallowed; also, it doesn't gum up your hair; also, if you want to take a cake of soap with you, all you have to look out for is that you don't lose the soap. Nobody tries to use toilet soap in sea-water more than once.

And surf-bathing! If there is a bigger swindle than surf-bathing, the United States Postal authorities haven't heard of it yet. It is all very well for the women. They can hang on to the ropes and squeal at the big waves and have a perfectly lovely time. Some of the really daring ones crouch down till they actually get their shoulder-blades wet. You have to see that for yourself to believe it, but it is as true as I am sitting here. They do so - some of them. But good land! There's no swimming in surf-bathing, no fun for a man. The water is all bouncing up and down. One second it is over head and hands, and the next second it is about to your knees, with a malicious undertow tickling your feet and tugging at your ankles; and growling: "Aw, you think you're some, don't you? Yes. Well, for half a cent wouldn't take you out and drown you,." And I don't like the looks of that boat patrolling up and down between the ropes and the raft. It is too suggestive, too like the skeleton at the banquet, too blunt a reminder that maybe what the undertow growls is not all a bluff.

Another drawback to the ocean as a swimming-hole is that the distances are all wrong. If you want to go to the other side of the "crick" you must take a steamboat. There is no such thing as bundling up your clothes and holding them out of water with one hand while you swim with the other, perhaps dropping your knife or necktie in transit. I have never been on the other side of the "crick" even on a steamboat, but I am pretty sure that there are no yellow-hammers' nests over there or watermelon patches. There were above the dam. At the seaside they give you as an objective point a raft, anchored at what seems only a little distance from where it gets deep enough to swim in, but which turns out to be a mighty far ways when the water bounces so. When you get there, blowing like a quarter-horse and weighing nine tons as you lift yourself out, there is nothing to do but let your feet hang over while you get rested enough to swim back. It wasn't like that above the dam.

I tell you the ocean is altogether too big. Some profess to admire it on that account, but it is my belief that they do it to be in style. I admit that on a bright, blowy day, when you can sit and watch the shining sails far out on the horizon's rim, it does look right nice, but I account for it in this way: it puts you in mind of some of these expensive oil paintings, and that makes you think it is kind of high class. And another thing: It recalls the picture in the joggerfy that proved the earth was round because the hull of a ship disappears before the sails, as it would if the ship was going over a hill. You sweep your eye along where the sky and water meet, and it seems you can note the curvature of the earth. Maybe it is that, and maybe it is all in your own eye. I am not saying.

There are good points, too, about the sea on a clear night when the moon is full; or when there is no moon, and the phosphorescence in the water shows, as if mermaids' children were playing with blue-tipped matches. I like to see it when a gale is blowing, and the white caps race. Yes, and when it is a flat calm, with here and there a tiny cat's-paw crinkling the water into gray-green crepe. And also when - but there! it is no use cataloguing all kinds of weather and all hours of the day and night. What I don't approve of in the ocean is its everlasting bigness. It is so discouraging. It makes a body seem so no-account and insignificant. You come away feeling meaner than a sheep-killing dog. "Oh, what's the use?" you say to yourself. "What's the use of my breaking my neck to do anything or be anybody? Before I was born - before History began - before any foot of being that could be called a man trod these sands, the waves beat thus the pulse of time. When I am gone - when all that man has made, that seems so firm and everlasting, shall have crumbled into the earth, whence it sprang, this wave, so momentary and so eternal, shall still surge up the slanting beach, and trail its lacy mantle in retreat . . . . O spare me a little, that I may recover my strength before I go hence, and be no more seen."

And that's no way for a man to feel. He ought to be confident and sure of himself. If he hasn't yet done all that he laid out to do, he should feel that it is in him to do it, and that he will before the time comes for him to go, and that when it is done it shall be orth while.

It is the ocean's everlasting bigness that makes it so cold to swim in. At the seaside bathing pavilions they have a blackboard whereon they chalk up "70" or "72" or whatever they think folks will like. They never say in so many words that a man went down into the water and held a thermometer in it long enough to get the true temperature, but they lead you to believe it. All I have to say is that they must have very optimistic thermometers. I just wish some of these poor little seashore boys could have a chance to try the Old Swimming-hole up above the dam. Certainly along about early going-barefoot time the water is a little cool, but you take it in the middle of August - ah, I tell you! When you come out of the water then you don't have to run up and down to get your blood in circulation or pile the warm sand on yourself or hunt for the steam-room. Only thing is, if you stay in all day, as you want to, it thins your blood, and you get the "fever 'n' ager." But you can stay in as long as you want to, that 's the point, without your lips turning the color of a chicken's gizzard.

And there's this about the Old Swimming-hole, or there was in my day: There were no women and girls fussing around aid squalling: "Now, you stop splashin' water on me! Quit it now! Quee-yut!" I don't think t looks right for women folks to have anything to do with water in large quantities. On a sail-boat, now, they are the very - but perhaps we had better not go into that. At a picnic, indeed, trey used to take off their shoes and stockings and paddle their feet in the water, but that was as much as ever they did. They never thought of going in swimming. Even at the seashore, now when Woman is so emancipated, they go bathing not swimming. I don't like to see a woman swim any more than I like to see a woman smoke a cigar. And for the same reason. It is more fun than she is entitled to. A woman's place is home minding the baby, and cooking the meals. Nothing would do her but she had to be born a woman, she had the same liberty of choice that we men had. Very well, I say, let her take the consequencies.

It is only natural, then, that she should refuse to let her boys go swimming. She pays off her grudge that way.

Just because she can't go herself she is bound the they shan't either. She says they will get drowned, but we know about that. It is only an excuse to keep them from having a little fun. She has to say something. They won't get drowned. Why, the idea! They haven't the least intention of any such thing.

"Well, but Robbie, supposing you couldn't help yourself?"

"How couldn't help myself?"

"Why, get the cramps. Suppose you got the cramps, then what?"

"Aw, pshaw! Cramps nothin'! They hain't no sich of a thing. And, anyhow, if I did get 'em, wouldn't jist kick 'em right out. This way."

"Now, Robbie, you know you did have a terrible cramp in your foot just only the other night. Don't you remember?"

"Aw, that! That ain't nothin'. That ain't the cramps that drownds people. Didn't I tell you wouldn't fist kick it right out? That's what they all do when they git the cramps. But they don't nobody git 'em now no more."

"I don't want you to go in the water and get drowned. You know you can't swim."

This is too much. Oh, this is rank injustice! Worse yet, it is bad logic.

"How 'm I ever goin' to learn if you don't let me go to learn?"

"Well, you can't go, and that's the end of it."

Isn't that just like a woman? Perfectly unreasonable! Dear! dear!

"Now, Ma, listen here. S'posin' we was all goin' some place on a steamboat, me and you and Pa and the baby and all of us, and - "

"That won't ever happen, I guess."

"CAN'T YOU LET ME TELL YOU? And s'posin' the boat was to sink, and I could swim and save you from drown - "

"You're not going swimming, and that's all there is about it."

"Other boys' mas lets them go. I don't see why I can't go."

No answer.

"Ma, won't you let me go? I won't get drowned, hope to die if I do. Ma, won't you let me go? Ma! Ma-a! - Maw-ah!"

"Stop yelling at me that way. Good land! Do you think I'm deaf?"

"Won't you let me go? Please, won't you let - "

"No, I won't. I told you I wouldn't, and I mean it. You might as well make up your mind to stay at home, for you're - not - going.

Hush up now. This instant, sir! Robbie, do you hear me? Stop crying. Great baby! wouldn't be ashamed to cry that way, as big as you are!"

Mean old Ma! Guess she'd cry too'f she could see the other kids that waited for him to go and ask her - if she could see them moving off, tired of waiting. They're 'most up to Lincoln Avenue.

"Oooooooooooo-hoo - hoo - hoo - hoohoooooooooo-ah! I wanna gow-ooooo."

"Did you hoe that corn your father told you to?"

"Oooooooooooo-hoo-hoo-hoo-ooooooooo! I wanna gow-ooooooo."

"Robbie! Did you hoe that corn?"

The last boy, the one with the stone-bruise on his heel, limps around the corner. They have all the fun. His ma won't let him go barefoot because it spreads his feet.

"Robbie! Answer me."

"Mam?"

"Did you hoe that corn your father told you to?"

"Yes mam."

"All of it? Did you hoe all of it?"

" Prett' near all of it." Well begun is half done. One hill is a good beginning, and half done is pretty nearly all.

"Go and finish it."

"I will if you'll let me go swimmin'."

It flashes upon him that even now by running he can catch up with the other fellows. He can finishing the hoeing when he gets back.

"You'll do it anyhow, and you're not going swimming. Now, that's the end of it. You march out to that garden this minute, or I'll take a stick to you. And don't let me hear another whimper out of you. Robbie! Come back here and shut that door properly. I shall tell your father how you have acted. wouldn't be ashamed - I'd be ashamed to show temper that way."

It says for children to obey their parents, but if more boys minded their mothers there would be fewer able to swim. While I shrink with horror from even seeming to encourage dropping the hoe when the sewing-machine gets to going good, by its thunderous spinning throwing up an impervious wall of sound to conceal retreat into the back alley, across the street, up the alley back of Alexander's, and so on up to Fountain Avenue in time to catch up with the gang, still I regard swimming as an exercise of the extremest value in the development of the growing boy. It builds up every muscle. It is particularly beneficial to the lungs. To have a good pair of lungs is the same thing as having a good constitution. It is nice to have a healthy boy, and it is nice to have an obedient boy, but if one must choose which he will have - that's a very difficult question. I think it should be left to the casuists. Nevertheless, now is the boy's only chance to grow. He will have abundant opportunities to learn obedience.

In the last analysis there are two ways of acquiring the art of swimming, the sudden way and the slow way. I have never personally known anybody that learned in the sudden way, but I have heard enough about it to describe it. It it's the quickest known method. One day the boy its among the gibbering white monkeys at the river's edge, content to splash in the water that comes but half way to his crouching knees. The next day he swims with the big boys as bold as any of them. In the meantime his daddy has taken him out in a boat, out where it is deep - Oh! Ain't it deep there? - and thrown him overboard. The boat is kept far enough away to be out of the boy's reach and yet near enough to be right there in case anything happens. (I like that "in case anything happens." It sounds so cheerful.) It being what Aristotle defines as "a ground-hog case," the boy learns to swim immediately. He has to.

It seems reasonable that he should. But still and all, I don't just fancy it. Once when a badly scared man grabbed me by the arms in deep water I had the fear of drowning take hold of my soul, and it isn't a nice feeling at all. Somehow when I hear folks praising up this method of teaching a child to swim, I seem to hear the little fellow's screams that he doesn't want to be thrown into the water. I can see him clinging to his father for protection, and finding that heart hard and unpitying. I can see his fingernails whiten with his clutch on anything that gives a hand-hold. His father strips off his grip, at first with boisterous laughter, and then with hot anger at the little fool. He calls him a cry-baby, and slaps his mouth for him, to stop his noise. The little body sprawls in the air and strikes with a loud splash, and the child's gargling cry is strangled by the water whitened by his mad clawings. I can see his head come up, his eyes bulging, and his face distorted with the awful fear that is ours by the inheritance of ages. He will sink and come up again, not three times, but a hundred times. Eventually he will win safe to shore, panting and trembling, his little heart knocking against his ribs, it is true, but lord of the water from that time forth. It is a very fine method, yes . . . but . . . well, if it was my boy I had just as lief he tarried with the little white monkeys at the river's edge. Let him squeal and crouch and splash and learn how to half drown the other fellow by shooting water at him with the heel of his hand. Let him alone. He will be watching the others swim. He will edge out a little farther and kick up his heels while with his hands he holds on the ground. He will edge out a little farther still and try to keep his feet on the bottom and swim with his hands. Be patient in his attempt to combine the two methods of travel. He is not the only one that fears to be one thing or the other, and regards a mixture of both as the safest way to get along.

No, I cannot say that I wholly approve of the sudden method of learning to swim. It has the advantange of lumping all the scares of a lifetime into one and having it over with, and yet I don't suppose the scare of being thrown into the water by one's daddy is really greater than being ducked in mid-stream by some hulking, cackle-voiced big boy. It seems greater though, I suppose, because a fellow cannot very well relieve his feelings by throwing stones at his daddy and bawling: "Goldarn you anyhow, you - you big stuff! I'll get hunk with you, now you see if I don't!" Here would be just the place to make the little boy tie knots in the big boy's shirt-sleeves, soak the knots in water, and pound them between stones. But that is kind of common, I think. They told about it at the swimming-hole above the dam, but nobody was mean enough to do it. Maybe they did it down at the Copperas Banks below town. The boys from across the tracks went there, a race apart, whom we feared, and who hated us, if the legend chalked up on the fences "DAMB THE PRODESTANCE," meant anything.

Under the slow method of learning to swim one had leisure to observe the different fashions - dog-fashion and cow-fashion, steamboat-fashion, and such. The little kids and beginners swam dog-fashion, which on that account was considered contemptible. The fellow was sneered at that screwed up his face as if in a cloud of suffocating dust, and fought the water with noise and fury, putting forth enough energy to carry him a mile, and actually going about two feet if he were headed down stream. Scientific men say that the use of the limbs, first on one side and then on the other, is instinctive to all creatures of the monkey tribe. That is the way they do in an emergency, since that is the way to scramble up among the tree limbs. I know that it is the easiest way to swim, and the least effective. When the arms are extended together in the breast stroke, it is as much superior to dogfashion as man is superior to the ape. I have always thought that to swim thus with steady and deliberate arm action, the water parting at the chin and rising just to the root of the underlip, was the most dignified and manly attitude the human being could put himself in. Cow-fashion was a burlesque of this, and the swimmer reared out of water with each stroke, creating tidal waves. It was thought to be vastly comic. Steamboat-fashion was where a fellow swam on his back, keeping his body up by a gentle, secret paddling motion with his hands, while with his feet he lashed the water into foam, like some river stern-wheeler. If he could cry: "Hoo! hoo! hoo!" in hoarse falsetto to mimic the whistle, it was an added charm.

It was a red-headed boy from across the tracks on his good behavior at the swimming-hole above the dam that I first saw swim hand-over-hand, or "sailor-fashion" as we called it, rightly or wrongly, I know not. I can hear now the crisp, staccato little smack his hand gave the water as he reached forward.

It has ever since been my envy and despair. It is so knowing, so "sporty." I class it with being able to wear a pink-barred shirt front with a diamond-cluster pin in it; with having my clothes so nobby and stylish that one thread more of modishness would be beyond the human power to endure; with being genuinely fond of horseracing; with being a first-class poker player, I mean a really first-class one; with being able to swallow a drink of whisky as if I liked it instead of having to choke it down with a shudder; with knowing truly great men like Fitzsimmons, or whoever it is that is great now, so as to be able to slap him on the back and say: "Why, hello! Bob, old boy, how are you?" with being delighted with the company of actors, instead of finding them as thin as tissue-paper - what wouldn't I give if I could be like that? My life has been a sad one. But I might find some comfort in it yet if I coin only get that natty little spat on the water when I lunge forward swimming overhand.

We used to think the Old Swimming-hole was a bully place, but I know better now. The sycamore leaned well out over the water, and there was a trapeze on the branch that grew parallel with the shore, but the water near it was never deep enough to dive into. And that is another occasion of humiliation. I can't dive worth a cent. When I go down to the slip behind Fulton Market - they sell fish at Fulton Market; just follow your nose and you can't miss it - and see the rows of little white monkeys doing nothing but diving, I realize that the Old Swimming-hole with all its beauties, its green leafiness, its clean, long grass to lie upon while drying in the sun, or to pull out and bite off the tender, chrome-yellow ends, was but a provincial, country-fake affair. There were no watermelon rinds there, no broken berry-baskets, no orange peel, no nothing. All the fish in it were just common live ones. And there was no diving. But at the real, proper city swimming-place all the little white monkeys can dive. Each is gibbering and shrieking: "Hey, Chim-meel Chimmee! Hey, Chim-mee! Chimmee! Hey, CHIM-MEEEE! How'ss t 'iss?" crossing himself and tipping over head first, coming up so as to "lay his hair," giving a shaking snort to clear his nose and mouth of water, regaining the ladder with three overhand strokes (every one of them with that natty little spat that I can't get), climbing up to the string-piece and running for Chimmy, red-eyed, shivering, and dripping, to ask: "How wass Cat?" And I can't dive for a cent - that is, I can't dive from a great elevation. I set my teeth and vow I just will dive from ten feet above the water, and every time it gets down to a poor, picayune dive off the lowest round of the ladder. I blame my early education for it. I was taught to be careful about pitching myself head foremost on rocks and broken bottles. I used to think it was a fine swimming-hole, and that I was having a grand, good time, well worth any ordinary licking; but now that I have traveled around and seen things, I know that it was a poor, provincial, country-jake affair after all. The first time I swam across and back without "letting down" it was certainly an immense place, but when I went back there a year ago last summer - why, pshaw! it wasn't anything at all. It was a dry summer, I admit, but not as dry as all that. A poor, pitiful, provincial, two-for-a cent - and yet . . .

and yet . . . And yet I sat there after I had dressed, and mused upon the former things - the life that was, but never could be again; the Eden before whose gate was a flaming sword turning every way. The night was still and moonless. The Milky Way slanted across the dark dome above. It was far from the street lamps that greened among the leafy maples in the silent streets. Gushes of air stirred the fluttering sycamore, and whispered in the tall larches that marched down the boundary line of the Blymire property. The last group of swimmers had turned into the road from around the clump of willows at the end of the pasture. The boy that is always the last one had nearly caught up with the others, for the velvet pat of his bare feet in the deep dust was slowing. Their eager chatter softened and softened, until it blended with the sounds of night that verge on silence, the fall of a leaf, the up-springing of a trodden tuft of grass, the sleepy twitter of a dreaming bird, and the shrilling of locusts patiently turning a creaking wheel. I heard the thump of hoofs and buggy wheels booming in the covered bridge, and a shudder came upon me that was not all the chill of falling dew. Again I was a little boy, standing in a circle of my fellows and staring at something pale, stretched out upon the ground. Ben Snyder had dived for It and found It and brought It up and laid It on the long, clean grass. Some one had said we ought to get a barrel and roll It on the barrel, but there was none there. And then some one said: "No, it was against the law to touch anything like That before the Coroner came." So, though we wished that something might be done, we were glad the law stepped in and stringently forbade us touching what our flesh crept to think of touching. No longer existed for us the boy that had the spy-glass and the "Swiss Family Robinson." Something cold and terrible had taken his place, something that could not see, and yet looked upward with unwinking eyes. The gloom deepened, and the dew began to fall. We could hear the boy that ran for the doctor whimpering a long way off. We wanted to go home, and yet we dared not. Something might get us. And we could not leave That alone in the dark with It's eyes wide open. The locusts in the grass turned and turned their creaking wheel, and the wind whispered in the tall larches. We heard the thump of hoofs and wheels booming in the covered bridge. It was the doctor, come too late. He put his head down to It's bosom (the cold trickled down our backs), and then he said it was too late. If we had known enough, he said, we might have saved him. We slunk away. It was very lonesome. We kept together, and spoke low. We stopped to hearken for a moment outside the house where the boy had lived that had the spy-glass and the 'Swiss Family Robinson." Some one had told his mother. And then, with a great and terrible fear within us, we ran each to his own home, swiftly and silently. We knew now why mother did not want us to go swimming.

But the next afternoon when Chuck Grove whistled in our back alley and held up two fingers, I dropped the hoe and went with him. It was bright daylight then, and that is different from the night.

THE FIREMEN'S TOURNAMENT

It isn't only Christmas that comes but once a year and when it comes it brings good cheer; it's any festival that is worth a hill of beans, High School Commencement, Fourth of July, Sunday-school excursion, Election' bonfire, Thanksgiving Day (a nice day and one whereon you can eat roast turkey till you can't choke down another bite, and pumpkin-pie, and cranberry sauce. Tell you!) - but about the best in the whole lot, and something the city folks don't have, is Firemen's Tournament. That comes once a year, generally about the time for putting up tomatoes.

The first that most of us know about it is when we see the bills up, telling how much excursion rates will be to our town from Ostrander and Mt. Victory, and Wapatomica, and New Berlin, and Foster's, and Caledonia, and Mechanicsburg - all the towns around on both the railroads. But before that there was the Citizens' Committee, and then the Executive Committee, and the Finance Committee, and the Committee on Press and Publicity, and Printing and Prizes, and Decorations and Badges, and Music, and Reception to Firemen, and Reception to Guests - as many committees as there are nails in the fence from your house to mine. And these committees come around and tell you that we want to show the folks that we've got public spirit in our town, some spunk, some git-up to us. We want our town to contrast favorably with Caledonia where they had the Tournament last year. We want to put it all over the Caledonia people (they think they're so smart), and we can do it, too, if everybody will take a-holt and help. Well, we want all we can get. We expect a pretty generous offer from you, for one. Man that has as pretty and tasty got-up store as you have, and does the business that you do, ought to show his appreciation of the town and try to help along . . . . Oh, anything you're a mind to give. 'Most anything comes in handy for prizes. But what we principally need is cash, ready cash. You see, there's a good deal of expense attached to an enterprise of this character. So many little things you wouldn't think of, that you've just got to have. But laws! you'll make it all back and more, too. We cackleate there'll be, at the very least, ten thousand people in town that day, and it's just naturally bound to be that some of them will do their trading.

Thank you very much. that's very handsome of you. Good day. (What are you growling about? Lucky to get five cents out of that man.)

The Ladies' Aid of Center Street M. E., has secured the store-room recently vacated by Rouse & Meyers, and is going to serve a dinner that day for the benefit of the Carpet Fund of their church and about time, too, I say. I like to broke my neck there a week ago last Sunday night, when our minister was away. Caught my foot in a hole in the carpet, and a little more and wouldn't have gone headlong. So, it's: "Why, I've been meaning for more than a year, to call on you, Mrs. - . Mrs. - (Let me look at my list. Oh, yes) Mrs. Cooper, but we've had so much sickness at home - you know my husband's father is staying with us at present, and he's been in very poor health all winter -and when it hasn't been sickness, it's been company. You know how it is. And it seemed as if I - just - could - not make out to get up your way. What a pretty little place you have! So cozy! I was just saying to Mrs. Thorpe here, it was so seldom you saw a really pretty residence in this part of town. We think that up on the hill, where we reside, you know, is about the handsomest . . . . Yes, there are a great many wealthy people live up there. The Quackenbushes are enormously wealthy. I was saying to Mrs. Quackenbush only the other day that I thought the hill people were almost too exclusive . . . . Yes, it is a perfectly lovely day . . . . Er - er - We're soliciting for the Firemen's Tournament - well, not for the Tournament exactly, but the Ladies' Aid are going to give a dinner that day for the Carpet Fund and we thought perhaps you'd like to help along . . . . Oh, any little thing, a boiled ham or - . . . Well, we shall want some cake, but we'd druther - or, at least, rawther - have something more substantial, don't you know, pie or pickles or jelly, don't you know. And will you bring it or shall I send Michael with the carriage for it? . . . . Oh, thank you! If you would. It would be so much appreciated. So sorry we couldn't make a longer stay, but now that we've found the way . . . . Yes, that's very true. Well, good-afternoon."

The lady of the house watches them as Michael inquires: "Whur next, mum?" and bangs the door of the carriage. Then she turns and says to herself: "Huh!" Mrs. Thorpe is that instant observing: "Did you notice that crayon enlargement she had hanging up? Wouldn't it kill you?" To which the other lady responds: "Well, between you and I, Mrs. Thorpe, if I couldn't have a real hand-painted picture I wouldn't have nothing at all."

The lady of the house bakes a cake. She'll show them a thing or two in the cake line. And while it is in the oven what does that little dev -, that provoking Freddie, do but see if he can't jump across the kitchen in two jumps. Fall? What cake wouldn't fall? Of course it falls. But it is too late now to bake another, and if they don't like it, they know what they can do. She doesn't know that she's under any obligation to them.

Mrs. John Van Meter hears Freddie say off the little speech his mother taught him - Oh, you may be sure she'd be there as large as life, taking charge of everything, just as if she had been one of the workers, when, to my certain knowledge, she hadn't been to one of the committee meetings, not a one. I declare I don't know what Mr. Craddock is thinking of to let her boss every body around the way she does - and she smiles and says: "It's all right. It's just lovely. Tell your mamma Mrs. Van Meter is ever and ever so much obliged to her. Isn't he a dear boy?" And when he is gone, she says: "What are we ever going to do with all this cake? It seems as if everybody has sent cake. And whatever possessed that woman to attempt a cake, I - can't imagine. Ts! ts! ts! H-well. Oh, put it somewhere. Maybe we can work it off on the country people. Mrs. Filkins, your coffee smells PERfectly grand! Perfectly grand. Do you think we'll have spoons enough?"

The Tournament prizes are exhibited in the windows of the leading furniture emporium at the corner of Main and Center, each with a card attached bearing the name of the donor in distinctly legible characters. Old man Hagerman has been mowing all the rag-weed and cuckle-burrs along the line of march, and the lawns have had an unusual amount of shaving and sprinkling. Out near the end of Center Street, the grandstand has been going up, tiers of seats rising from each curb line. The street has been rolled and sprinkled and scraped until it is in fine condition for a running track. Why don't you pick up that pebble and throw it over into the lot? Suppose some runner should slip on that stone and fall and hurt himself, you'd be to blame.

The day before the Tournament, they hang the banner:

"WELCOME VOLUNTEER FIREMEN"

from Case's drugstore across to the Furniture Emporium. Along the line of march you may see the man of the house up on a step-ladder against the front porch, with his hands full of drapery and his mouth full of tacks. His wife is backing toward the geranium bed to get a good view, cocking her head on one side.

" How 'v vif?" he asks as well as he can for the tacks.

"Little higher. Oh, not so much. Down a little. Whope! that's. . . . Oh, plague take the firemen! Just look at that! Mercy! Mercy!"

The man of the house can't turn his head.

"Oh, I wouldn't have had it happen for I don't know what! Ts! Ts! Ts! That lovely silverleaf geranium that Mrs. Pritchard give me a slip of. Broke right off! Oh, my! My! My! Do you s'pose it'd grow if I was to stick it into the ground just as it is with all them buds on it?"

The man of the house lets one end of the drapery go and empties his mouth of tacks into his disengaged hand.

"I don't know. Ow! jabbed right into my gum! But I can tell you this: If you think I'm going to stick up on this ladder all morning while you carry on about some fool old geranium that you can just as well fuss with when I'm gone, why, you're mighty much mistaken."

"Well, you needn't take my head off. I feel awful about that geranium."

"Well, why don't you look where you're going? Is this right?"

"Yes, I told you. I wish now I'd done it myself. I can't ask you to do a thing about the house but there's a row raised right away."

People that don't want to go to the trouble of tacking up these alphabet flags on the edge of the veranda eaves (it takes fourteen of them to spell "WELCOME FIREMEN"), say they think a handsome flag - a really handsome one, not one of these twenty-five centers - is as pretty and rich looking a decoration as a body can put up.

Tents are raised in the vacant lots along Center Street, and counters knocked together for the sale of ice-cold lemonade, lemo, lemo, lemo, made in the shade, with a spade, by an old maid, lemo, lemo. Here y' are now, gents, gitch nice cool drink, on'y five a glass. There is even the hook for the ice-cream candy man to throw the taffy over when he pulls it. I like to watch him. It makes me dribble at the mouth to think about it.

The man that sells the squawking toys and the rubber balloons on sticks is in town. All he can say is:," Fi' cent." He will blow up the balloons tomorrow morning. The men with the black-velvet covered shields, all stuck full of "souvenirs," are here, and the men with the little canes. I guess we'll have a big crowd if it doesn't rain. What does the paper say about the weather?

The boys have been playing a new game for some time past, but it is only this evening that you notice it. The way of it is this: You take an express-wagon - it has to have real wheels: these sawed-out wheels are too baby - and you tie a long rope to the tongue and fix loops on the rope, so that the boys can put each a loop over his shoulder. (You want a good many boys.) And you get big, long, thick pieces of rag and you take and tie them so as to make a big, big, long piece, about as long as from here to 'way over there. And you lay this in the wagon, kind of in folds like. Then you go up to where they water the horses and two of you go at the back end of the wagon and the rest put the loops over their shoulders, and one boy says, "Are you ready ?" and he has a Fourth of July pistol and he shoots off a cap. And when you hear that, you run like the dickens and the two boys behind the wagon let out the hose (the big, long, thick piece of rag) and fix it so it lies about straight on the ground. And when you have run as far as the hose will reach, the boy with the Fourth of July pistol says: "Twenty-eight and two-fifths," and that's the game. And the kids don't like for big folks to stand and watch them, because they always make fun so.

In other towns they have Boys' Companies organized strictly for Tournament purposes. There was talk of having one here. Mat. King, the assistant chief, was all for having one so that we could compete in what he calls " the juveline contests , " but it fell through somehow.

Along about sun-up you hear the big farm-wagons clattering into town, chairs in the wagon bed, and Paw, and Maw, and Mary Elizabeth, and Martin Luther, and all the family, clean down to Teedy, the baby. He's named after Theodore Roosevelt, and they have the letter home now, framed and hanging up over the organ. But for all the wagon is so full, there is room for a big basket covered with a red-ended towel. (Seems to me I smell fried chicken, don't you?)

I just thought I'dt see if you'd bite. You've formed your notions of country people from "The Old Homestead" and these by-gosh-Mirandy novels. The real farmers, nowadays, drive into town in double-seated carriages with matched bays, curried so that you can see to comb your hair in their glossy sides. The single rigs sparkle in the sun, conveying young men and young women of such clean-cut, high-bred features as to make us wonder. And yet I don't know why we should wonder, either. They all come from good old stock. The young fellows run a little too strongly to patent-leather shoes and their horses are almost too skittish for my liking, but the girls are all right. If their clothes set better than you thought they would, why, you must remember that they subscribe for the very same fashion magazines that you do, and there is such a thing as a mail-order business in this country, even if you aren't aware of it.

All the little boys in town are out with their baskets chanting sadly:

PEANUTS? FIVE A BAG

You 'll hear that all day long.

But there isn't much going on before the excursion trains come in. Then things begin to hop. The grand marshal and his aides gallop through the streets as if they were going for the doctor. The trains of ten and fifteen coaches pile up in the railroad yard, and the yardmaster nearly goes out of his mind. People are so anxious to get out of the cars, in which they have been packed and jammed for hours, that they don't mind a little thing like being run over by a switching engine. Every platform is just one solid chunk of summer hats and babies and red shirts and alto horns. They have been nearly five hours coming fifty miles. Stopped at every station and sidetracked for all the regular trains. Such a time! Lots of fun, though. The fellows got out and pulled flowers, and seed cucumbers, and things and threw them at folks. You never saw such cut-ups as they are. Pretty good singers, too. Good part of the way, they sung "My Bonnie Lies Over the Ocean," and "How Can I Bear to Leave Thee," nice and slow, you know, a good deal of tenor and not much bass, and plenty of these" minor chords." (Yes, I know, some people call them "barber-shop chords," but I think "minor" is a nicer name.)

The band played "Hiawatha" eighteen times. One old fellow got on at Huntsville, and he says, to Joe Bangs (that's the leader), "Shay," he says, "play 'Turkey in er Straw,' won't you? Aw, go on. Play it. Thass goof feller. Go on."

Joe, he never heard of the tune. Don't you know it? Goes like this: . . . No, that ain't it. That's "Gray Eagle." Funny, I can't think how that tune starts. Well, no matter. They played an arrangement that had "Old Zip Coon" in it.

"Naw," he says, "tha' ain' it 't all. Go on. Play it. Play 'Turkey in er Straw.' Ah, ye don't know it. Thass reason. Betch don' know it. Don' know 'Turkey in er Straw!' Ho! Caw seff ml-m' sishn. Ho! You - you - you ain' no m'sishn. You - you you're zis bluff." Only about half-past eight, too. Think of that! So early in the morning. Ah me! That's one of the sad features of such an occasion.

If there is anything more magnificent than a firemen's parade, I don't know what it is. The varnished woodwork on the apparatus looks as if it had just come out of the shop and every bit of bright work glitters fit to strike you blind. You take, now, a nice hose-reel painted white and striped into panels with a fine red line, every other panel fruits and flowers, and every other panel a piece of looking-glass shaped like a cut of pie and; I tell you, it looks gay. That's what it does. It looks gay. Some of the hook-and-ladder trucks are just one mass of golden-rod and hydrangeas, and some of them are all fixed with this red-white-and-blue paper rope, sort of chenille effect, or more like a feather boa. Everybody has on white cotton gloves, and those entitled to carry speaking trumpets have bouquets in the bells of them, salvias, and golden-rod, and nasturtiums, and marigolds, and all such.

The Wapatomicas always have a dog up on top of their wagon. First off, you would think it didn't help out much, it is such a forlorn looking little fice; but this dog, I want you to know, waked up the folks late one night, 'way 'long about ten or eleven o'clock, barking at a fire. Saved the town, as you might say. And after that, the fire-boys took him for a mascot. I guess he didn't belong to anybody before. And another wagon has a chair on it, and in that chair the cutest little girl you almost eyer saw, hair all frizzed at the ends, and a wide blue sash and her white frock starched as stiff as a milk-pail. Everybody says: "Aw, ain't she just too sweet ?"

The Caledonias have tried to make quite a splurge this year. They walk four abreast, with their arms locked, and their white gloves on each other's shoulders. Their truck has on it what they call "an allegorical figure." There is a kind of a business (looks to me like it is the axle and wheels of a toy wagon, stood up on end and covered with white paper muslin and a string tied around the middle) that is supposed to be an hour-glass. Then there is a scythe covered with cotton batting, and then a man in a bath-robe (I saw the figure of the goods when the wind blew it open) also covered with white cotton batting. The man has a wig and beard of wicking. First, I thought it was Santa Claus, and then I saw the scythe and knew it must be old Father Time. The hour-glass puzzled me no little though. The man has cotton batting wings. One of them is a little wabbly, but what can you expect from Caledonia? They're always trying to butt the bull off the bridge. They're jealous of our town. Oh, they stooped to all the mean, underhanded tricks you ever heard of to get the canning factory to go to their place instead of here. But we know a thing or two ourselves. Yes, we got the canning factory, all right, all right.

Did you notice how neat and trim our boys looked? None of this flub-dub of scarlet shirts with a big white monogram on the breast, or these fawn-colored suits with querlycues of braid all over. They spot very easily. And did you notice how the Caledonias had long, lean men walking with short, fat men, and nobody keeping step? Our boys were all carefully graded and matched, and their dark blue uniforms with just the neat nickel badge, I think, presented the best appearance of all. And I'll tell you another thing. They'll put it all over the Caledonias this afternoon. They won't let 'em get a smell.

Don't you like the fife-and-drum corps? The fifes set my teeth on edge, but I could follow the drums all day with their:

> Tucket a brum, brum brum-brum, tuck-all de brum
> Tucket a brum-brum, tuck-all de brum-brum-brum
> Tucket a blip-blip-blip-blip, tucka tuck-all de brum,
> Tucket a brum-brum, tuck-all de brum-brum-brum!

Part of the time the drummers click their sticks together instead of hitting the drum-head. That's what makes it sound so nice. I wish I could play the snare-drum.

In the Mechanicsburg band is a boy about fourteen years old, a muscular, sturdy chunk of a lad. He walks with his heels down, his calves bulged out behind, his head up, and the regular, proper swagger of a bandsman. He hasn't any uniform, but he's all right. He plays a solo B part, and he and the other solo cornet spell each other. On the repeat of every strain my boy rests, and rubs his lips with his forefinger, while he looks at the populace with bright, expectant eyes. When he blows, he scowls, and brings the cushion of muscle on the point of his chin clear up to his under lip, and he draws his breath through the corners of his mouth. He's the real thing. Bright boy, too, I judge, the kind that has a quick answer for everybody, like: "Aw, go chase yerself," or "Go on, yeh big stiff." Watch him on the countermarch when they pass the Radnor cornet band. The Radnors broke up the Mechanicsburg band last year and they're going to try to do it again this year. The musicians blow themselves the color of a huckleberry, and the drummers grit their teeth, and try to pound holes in their sheep-skins. Aha! It's the Radnor band got rattled in its time this year. Went all to pieces. The boy snatches, a rest. "Yah!" he squawks. "Didge ever get left?" and picks up the tune again. I wish I could play the cornet. Wouldn't play solo B or I wouldn't play any - Ooooooooh! Did you see that? Took that stick by the other end from the knob and slung it away, 'way up in the air, whirling like sixty, and caught it when it came down and never missed a step. Look at him juggle it from hand to hand, over his shoulder, and behind his back, and under one leg, whirling so fast that you can hardly see it, and all in perfect step. Whope! I thought he was going to drop it that time but he didn't. That's something you don't see in the cities. There, all the drum-major does with his stick is just to point it the way the band is to go. I like our fashion the best. Geeminentally! Look at that! I bet it went up in the air forty feet if it went an inch. I wish I was a drummajor. I guess I'd sooner be a drum-major than anything else. Oh, well, detective - that's different.

Let's go farther along. Don't get too near the judges' stand. I know. It's the best place to see the finish of an event, but I've been to Firemen's Tournament before. You let me pick out the seats. Up close to the judges' stand is all right till you come to the 'wet races." What? Oh, you wait and see. Fun? Well, I should say so. Hope they'll clear all those boys off the rail. Here! Get down off that rail. Think we can see through you? You're thin, but you're not thin enough for that. Yes, I mean you, and don't you give me any of your impudence either. Look at those women out there.

Right spang in the way of the scraper. Isn't that a woman all over? A woman and a hen, I don't know which is - Well, hel-lo! Where'd you come from? How's all the folks? Where's Lizzie? Didn't she come with you? Aw, isn't that too bad? Scalding hot! Ts! Ts! Ts! Seems as if they made preserving kettles apurpose so's they'd tip up when you go to pour anything . . . . Why, I guess we can. Move over a little, Charley. Can you squeeze in? That's all right. Pretty thick around here, isn't it? There's the band starting up. About time, I think. Teedle-eedle umtum, teedle-eedle, um-tum. "Hiawatha,"of course. What other tune is there on earth? I've got so I know almost all of it.

First is - let me see the program. First is what Mat. King calls "the juveline contest." It says here: "Run with truck carrying three ladders one hundred yards. Take fifteen-foot ladder from truck, raise it against structure" - that's the judges' stand - "and boy ascend. Time to be taken when climber grasps top rung of ladder." They're off. That pistol-shot started them. Why can't people sit down? See just as well if they did. New Berlin's, I guess. Pretty good. He's hanging out the slate with the time on it. Eighteen and four-fifths. Oh, no, never in the world. Here's the Mt. Victory boys. See that light-haired boy. Go it, towhead! Ah, they've got the ladder crooked. Eighteen. That's not so bad. . . . Oh, quit your fooling. He's nothing of the kind. Honestly? What! that old skeezicks? Who to, for pity's sake? Well, I thought he was a confirmed old bachelor, if anybody ever was. Well, sir, that just goes to show that any man, I don't care who he is, can get married if he - Who were those? Are those the Caledonia juveniles? I don't think much of 'em, do you? Seventeen and two-fifths. I wouldn't have thought it. So their team gets the first prize. Well, we weren't in that.

What's next? "First prize, silver water-set, donated by Hon. William Krouse." Since when did old Bill Krouse get to be "Honorable?" Yes, well, don't talk to me about Bill Krouse. I know him and his whole connection and there isn't an honest hair - "Association trophy will also be competed for." Oh, that's the goldlined loving cup we saw in the window. Our boys have won it twice and the Caledonias have won it twice. If we get it this time, it will be ours for keeps. "Run with truck one hundred and fifty yards; take twenty-five foot ladder," and so forth and so forth, Dan O'Brien's the boy for scaling ladders. He was going to enlist in the Boer War, he hates the English so. Down on them the worst way. And say, what do you think? Last year, at Caledonia, he won the first prize for individual ladder scaling. And what do you suppose the first prize was? A picture of Queen Victoria. Isn't that Caledonia all over? there's a kind of rivalry between our boys and the Caledonias.

Here they come now. Those are the Caledonian. Tell by the truck . . . . Do you think so? I don't think they're anything so very much. Nix. You'll never do it. Look at the way they run with their heads up. That shows they're all winded. Look at the clumsy way they got the ladder off the wagon. Blap! The judge thought it was coming through the boards on him. Oh, pretty good, pretty good, but you just wait till you see our boys. Look at the fool hanging there on the ladder waiting till the time is announced. Isn't that Caledonia all over? Yah! Come down! Come down! What is it? Twenty-five seconds. What's the record? Twenty-four and four-fifths? Oh, well, it isn't so bad for Caledonia, but you just wait and see what our boys do. Hear those yaps from Caledonia yell! If there's anything I despise it is for a man to whoop and holler and make a public spectacle of himself. Who's this? Oh, the Radnors. They're out of it. Look at them. Pulling every which way. That ladder's too straight up and down. Twenty-seven and two-fifths. What did I tell you? . . . What time does your train go? Well, why don't you and your wife come take supper with us? Why didn't you look us up noon-time? . . . I could have told you better than that. (They went to the Ladies' Aid dinner.) Well, we shan't have much, I expect, but we'll try and scrape up something more filling than layer-cake. The idea of expecting to feed hungry people on layer-cake! It's an imposition . . . . I didn't notice which one it was. Doesn't matter any way. Only twenty-eight. Ah, here are our boys. They've got blue silk running-breeches on. Well, maybe it is sateen. Let the women folks alone for knowing sateen from silk a mile off. How much a yard did you say it was? Notice the way they start with their hands on the ground, just like the pictures on the sporting page of the Sunday newspapers. Here they come. Oh, I hope they'll win. That's Charley Rodehaver in front. Run! Oh, why don't you run? Come on! Come on! Come on! Come on! COME ON! COME ON! COME O - O-oh! See Dan skip up that ladder! Go it, Dan! Go it, old boy! Hooray-ay! Hooray-ay, ay! What's the time? Twenty-four! Twenty- four flat! BROKE THE RECORD! Hooray-ay-ay! Where's Caledonia now? Where's Caledonia now? Oh, I'm so glad our boys won. There goes the Caledonia chief. I'll bet he feels like thirty cents, Spanish. Ya-a-a-ah! Ya-a-a-ah! Where's Caledonia now? They can't beat that, the other fellows can't, and it's our trophy for keeps . . . . Oh, some crank in the next row. "Wouldn't I please sit down and not obstruct the view." Guess he comes from Caledonia.

Looks like it. You stand up, too, why don't you? Those planks are terribly hard . . . . I didn't notice. Yes, that wasn't so bad. Twenty-five and two-fifths. But it's our trophy. There goes Dan now. Hey, Dan! Good boy, Dan! Wave your handkerchief at him. Hooray-ay-ay! Good boy, Dan!

Next is a wet race. Now look out. Let's see what the program says: "Run seventy-five yards to structure, on top of which an empty barrel has been placed with spout outlet near top. Barrel to be filled with water by means of buckets from reservoir" - That big tin-lined box opposite is the reservoir. They are filling it now with a hose attached to the water-plug yonder - "until water issues from spout." What are they all laughing at? Which one? Oh, but isn't she mad? Talk about a wet hen. Why, Charley, the hose got away from the man that was filling the reservoir and the lady was splashed. Why don't you use your eyes and see what's going on and not be bothering me to tell you? Ip! There it goes again. Oh, ho! ho! ho! hee! hee! didn't I tell you it would be fun? See it run out of his sleeves . . . . I always get to coughing when I laugh as hard as that. Oh, dear me! Makes the tears come.

These are the fellows from Luxora. Oh, the clumsy things! Let the ladder get away from them, and it fell and hit that man in the second row right on the head. Hope it didn't hurt him much. See 'em scurry with the water buckets. Aw, get a move on! Get a move! Why, what makes them so slow? "Water, water!" Well, I should think as much. Not for themselves though. Those fellows at the bottom of the ladder are catching it, aren't they? Oh, pshaw, they don't mind it. They get it worse than that at a real fire when they aren't half so well fixed for it. Why, is there no bottom to that barrel at all? Why, look! . . . Say, the judge forgot to close the valve. There's a hose connected with the bottom of the barrel to run the water off after each trial and he's forgotten to - . . . Well, isn't that too bad! All that work for nothing. I suppose they'll let them try it over again . . . . That man must have got a pretty hard rap. They're carrying him out. His head's all bloody . . . Wapatomicas, I guess. Yes, Wapatomicas. I hope the valve's closed this time. Whope! did you see that? One fellow got hit with a water bucket and it was about half-full. It's running out of the spout. Yes, and it's falling on those people right where you wanted to sit. Hear the girls squeal. Talk about your fun. I don't want any better fun than this. Look at 'em come down the ladder just holding the sides with their hands. They couldn't do that if the ladder was dry.

Ah, here's our crowd. Come on! Come on! Come on! COME ON! Oh, don't be so slow with those buckets! Aren't they fine? Say, they don't care if they do spill a drop or two. Why. Why, what are they coming down for? It isn't running out of the spout yet. Come back! COME BACK! Oh, pshaw! Just threw it away by being in too much of a hurry. That judge looks funny, doesn't he, with a rubber overcoat on and the sun shining? See, he's telling them: "One bucket more." They'll let 'em have another trial, of course . . . . No? Oh, that's an outrage. That' s not fair. The Caledonias will get it now. . . . Yes, sir, they did get it. Oh, well, accidents will happen. What? "Where's Caledonia now?" Well, they got it by a fluke. What say? . . . Well only for - Oh, pshaw! Now, don't tell me that because I was there and - Well, I say they didn't . . . . I know better, they didn't . . . . Oh, shut up. You don't know what you're talking about. I tell you - Now, Mary, don't you interfere. I'm not quarreling. I'm just telling this gentleman back of me that - Well, all right, if you're going to cry. If there was any fouling done it was the Caledonias that did it, though.

The next is where they "run three hundred feet from the judges' stand, raise ladder, hose company to couple to hydrant, break coupling in hose and put on nozzle, scale ladder, and fill twenty-five gallon barrel." Only the Caledonias. and our boys are entered in this. Now we'll see which is the best. All right, Mary, I won't say a word . . . . Say, for country-jakes, those Caledonias didn't do so badly. I give them that much. Look at the water fly! I'll bet those folks near the judges' stand wish they'd brought their umbrellas. Now you see why these are the best seats, don't you? I told you I'd been to Firemen's Tournaments before. What? You'll have to talk louder than that if you want me to hear with all this noise . . . . Oh, that'll be all right. They'll be so hungry they won't notice it.

Here, be careful how you wabble that hose around. Good thing they turned the water off at the plug just when they did or we'd have been - Here's our company. Where's Caledonia now? Eh? Pretty work! Pretty work! Say, do you know that hose full of water's heavy? Now watch Riley. Riley's the one that's got the nozzle. Always up to some monkeyshine. Ah! See him? See him? Oh, is n"t he soaking them? Oh-ho! Ho! Ho! ha! ha! hee-hee! Yip.

Blame clumsy fool! . . . P-too! Yes, in my mouth and in my ears and down the back of my neck. All over. Running out of my sleeves. Everything I got on is just ruined. Completely ruined. Come on. Let's go home. There's nothing more to see, much. Aw, come on. Well, stay if you want to, but I'm going home, and get some dry clothes on me. You get me to go to another Firemen's Tournament and you'll know it. Look at that monkey from Caledonia laughing at me. For half a cent I'd go up and smack his face for him . . . . Aw, let up on your "Where's Caledonia now?" Give us a rest. Well, are you coming, you folks? . . . Kind of a fizzle this year, wasn't it?

However, after supper, with dry clothes on, it isn't so bad. The streets are packed. All the firemen are parading and shouting: "Who? Who? Who are we?" The Caledonias got one more prize than our boys. Well, why shouldn't they? Entered in three more events. I don't see as that's anything to brag of or to carry brooms about. All the fife-and-drum corps are out, and the bands are all playing "Hiawatha" at once, but not together. Not all either. There's one band in front of Hofmeyer's playing "Oh, Happy Day! That Fixed my Choce." That's funny: to play a hymn-tune in front of a beer-saloon. Hofmeyer seems to think it's all right. He's inviting them in to have something. "Took the hint?" I don't understand . . . . Oh, is that so? I didn't know there were other words to that tune.

See that woman with four little ones. Her husband's carrying two more. "I want to go howm. Why cain't we gow howm? I do' want to gow howm pretty soon. I want to gow na-ow!" Eh, Mary, how would you like to lug them around all day and then stand up in the cars all the way home?

Well, good-by. Hope you had a nice time. Give my regards to all the folks. Don't be in such a rush, my friend . . . . Oh, did you see? It must be the man that got hit on the head with the ladder. Taking him home on a stretcher. Gee! That's tough. Skull fractured, eh?

Dear! Dear! I hear they have been keeping company a long time, and were to have been married soon. No wonder she cried and took on so. Poor girl! Yes, it's the women that suffer . . . . Oh, quite a day for accidents. I didn't mind, though, after I had changed my clothes. I took some quinine, and I guess I'll be all right. Lucky you got a seat. Well, you're off at last. Good-by. Remember me to all. Good-by.

Well, thank goodness, that's over. Another ten minutes of them and wouldn't have - Well, Mary, what else could I do but ask them home after he told me what they didn't have to eat at the Ladies' Aid? . . . It was all right. Plenty good enough. Better than they have at home and I'll bet on it. The table looked beautiful. I'm glad the Tournament doesn't come but once a year. I'm about ready to drop.

THE DEVOURING ELEMENT

Mr. Silverstone was gloomily considering whether he had not better blow out the lights in the New York One Price Clothing Store, and lock up for the night. Kerosene was fifteen cents a gallon, and not a customer had been in since supper-time. Business was "ofle, simbly ofle."

The streets were empty. There were lights only in the barber shop where one patron was being lathered while two mandolins and a guitar gave a correct imitation of two house-flies and a bluebottle in Riley's where, in default of other occupation, Mr. Riley was counting up; in Oesterle's, where a hot discussion was going on as to whether Christopher Columbus was a Dutchman or a Dago, and in Miller's, where Tom Ball was telling Tony, who impassively wiped the perforated brass plate let into the top of the bar, that he, Tom Ball, "coul' lick em man ill Logan coun'y."

Lamps shone in every parlor, where little girls labored with: "And one and two, three and one and two, three," occasionally coming out to look at the clock to see if the hour was any nearer being up than it was five minutes ago. They also shone in sitting-rooms, where boys looked fiercely at "$X2 + 2Xy + y2$," mothers placidly darned stockings, and fathers, Weekly Examiner in hand, patiently struggled to disengage

Eugene Wood

from "boiler-plate" and bogus news about people snatched from the jaws of death by the timely use of Dr. McKinnon's Healing Extract of Timothy and Red-top, items of real news, such as who was sick and what ailed them, who cut his foot with the ax while splitting stove-wood, and where the cake sale by the Rector's Aid of Grace P.E. would be held next week.

At the prayer-meeting, Uncle Billy Nicholson was giving in his experience and had just got to that part about: "Sometimes on the mountaintop, and sometimes in the valley, but still, nevertheless - " when, all of a sudden, something happened,

The mandolins stopped with a jerk. Mr. Riley stood tranced at: "And ten is thirty-five." Mr. Ball was stricken dumb in the celebration of his own great physical powers. The crowd in Oesterle's forgot Columbus, and were as men beholding a ghost. The drowsy congregation sat up rigid, and Mr. Silverstone gave a guilty start. He had been thinking of that very thing!

The next instant, front doors were wrenched open, and the street echoed with the sound of windows being raised. Fathers and sons rushed out on the front porch, followed by little girls, to whom any excuse to stop practising was like a plank to a drowning man.

They had heard aright. Up by the Soldiers' Monument fell the clump of tired feet, and upon the air floated the wild alarm of -.

"FIRE! Pooh-ha! FIRE! Poof! FIRE!"

Mat King, the assistant chief, kicked off his slippers,

and swiftly laced up his shoes, grabbed his speaking-trumpet and his helmet, and tore out of the house. If he could only get to the engine-house before Charley Lomax, the chief! But Charley was the lone customer in the barber's char. With the lather on one side of his face, he clapped on his hat and broke for the firebell, four doors below.

"Where's it at?"

"FIRE! Pooh-ha! FIRE! Sm-poohl Fi- (gulp) - FIRE!"

"It's Linc Hoover. Hay, Linc! Where's the fire?"

"FIRE! Pooh-ha! FIRE! ha, ha! FIRE!"

"Hay, Linc! Where's it at? Tell me and I'll run. Hay! Where's it at?"

"FIRE! Swope's be - (gulp) Swope's barn. FIRE!"

"Which Swope? Henry or the old man?"

"FIRE! Pooh! J. K. Swope. Whoo-ha, whooh-ha! Out out on West End Avenue. Poof!"

The news thus being passed, the fresher runners scampered ahead, bawling: "FOY-URRR' FOY-URRR! and Linc, the hero, slowed down, gasping for breath and spitting cotton.

"Whew!" he whistled, gustily, his arms dropping and his whole frame collapsing. "Gee! I'm 'bout tuckered. Sm-pooh! Sm-pooh! Run all th' way f'm - sm-ha, sm-ha! - run all th' way f'm - mouth's all stuck together - p'too ! ha ! Pooh ! Fm West End Avenue and

Swo - Swope's. Gee! I'm hot's flitter."

"Keep y' coat on when you're all of a prespiration, that way. How'd it ketch ?"

" Count know. 'S comin' by there an' I - whoof! I smelt smoke and - Gosh! I'm all out o' breath - an' I looked an' I je-e-est could see a light - wisht I had a drink o' somepin' to rench mum mouth out. Whew! Oh, laws! An' it was Swope's barn and I run in an' opened the door, didn't stop to knock or nung, an' I hollered out: 'Yib barn's afire!' an' he run out in his sockfeet, an' he says: 'My Lord!' he says. 'Linc,' he says, 'run git the ingine an' I putt." Linc drew in a long, tremulous breath like a man that has looked on sorrow.

"Why 'n't you - "

"Betchy 't was tramps," interrupted a bystander. "Git in the haymow an' think they got to have their blamed old pipe a-goin' -"

"Cigarettes, more likely," said another. "More darn devilment comes from cigarettes -"

"Why'n't you - "

"Ount know nung 'bout tramps," said Linc. "All I seen was the fire. I was a-comin' long a-past there an' I smelt the smoke an' thinks I - What say?"

"Why'n't you telefoam down?"

Linc, the hero, shrunk a foot. "I gosh!" he admitted, "I never thought to."

" Jist'a' telefoamed, you could 'a' saved yourself all that - "

"Ain't they weltin' the daylights out o' that bell? All foolishness! Now they're ringin' the number - one, two, three, four. Yes, sir, that's up in the West End. You goin'? Come on, then."

"No, Frank, I can't let you go. You've got your lessons to get. Well, now, mother, make up your mind if you're comin' along. Cora, what on earth are you doing out here in the night air with nothing around you? Now, you mosey right back into that parlor, and don't you make a move off that piano-stool till your hour's up. Do you hear me? No. Frank. I told you once you couldn't go and that ends it. Stop your whining! I can't have you running hither and yon all hours of the night, and we not know where you are. Well, hurry up, then, mother. Take him in with you. Oh, just throw a shawl over your head. Nobody 'll see you, or if they do they won't care." The apparatus trundles by, the bells on the trucks tolling sadly as the striking gear on the rear axle engages the cam. A hurrying throng scuffles by in the gloom. The tolling grows fainter, the throng thinner.

"Good land! Is she going to be all night? Wish 't I hadn't proposed it. That's the worst of taking a woman anyplace. Fuss and fiddle by the hour in front of the looking-glass. Em! (Be all over by the time we get there) Oh, Em! Em! . . . EM! (Holler my head off!) EM! . . . . "Well, why don't you answer me? Well, I didn't hear you. How much long - Oh, I know about your 'minute.' 'Hour' you mean . . . . Oh, how do you do, Mrs. Conklin? Hello, Fred. Pleased to meet you, Miss Shoemaker. Yes, I saw in the paper you were visiting your sister. This your first visit to our little burg? Yes, we think it's quite a place. You see, we're trying to make your stay as interesting as possible . . . . Oh, no, not altogether on your account. No, no. Ha! Ha-ha-ha! Hum! ah! . . . Well, yes, if she ever gets done primping up. Oh, there you are. Miss Shoemaker, let me make you acquainted with my wife. Now, you girls'll have to get a move on if you want to see anything."

The male escorts grasp the ladies' arms and shove them ahead, that being the only way if you are ever going to get any place. The women gasp and pant and make a great to-do.

"Ooh! Wait till I get my breath. Will! Weeull! Don't go so fay-ust! Oooh! I can't stand it. Oh, well, you're a man."

But when they turn the corner that gives them a good view of the blaze, fluttering great puffs of flame, and hear the steady crackle and snapping, as it were, of a great popper full of pop-corn, they, too, catch the infection, and run with a loud swashing and slatting of skirts, giggling and squealing about their hair coming down.

In the waving orange glare the crowd is seen, shifting and moving. It seems impossible for the onlookers to remain constant in one spot. The chief, Charley Lomax, is gesticulating with wide arm movements. He puts his speaking-trumpet to his mouth. "Yoffemoffemoffemoffemoffi" he says.

"Wha-at?" the men halloo back.

"Yoffemoffemoffemoffemoff."

"What'd he say?"

"Search me. John, you run over and ask him what he wants. Or, no; I'll go myself."

"Why in Sam Hill didn't you come sooner?" demands the angry chief.

"Well, why in Sam Hill don't you talk so 's a body can understand you? 'Yoffemoffemoffemoffem.' Who can make sense out o' that?"

"The hose ain't long enough to reach from here to the hydrant. You 'n' some more of 'em run down t' th' house an' git that other reel."

"Aw, say, Chief! Look here. I'm awful busy right now. Can't somebody else go?"

"You go an' do what I tell you to, and don't gimme none o' your back talk."

(Too dag-gon bossy and dictatorial, that Charley Lomax is. Getting 'most too big for his breeches. Never mind. there's going to be a fire election week from Tuesday. See whether he'll be chief next year or not. Sending a man away from the fire right at the most interesting part!)

"I'll go, Chief, wommetoo," puts in jumbo Lee, all in a huddle of words. "Ije slivsnot. Aw ri. Mon Jim. Shoonmeansmore of 'em go gitth'otherreel."

Jumbo isn't a member of the fire department, though he is wild to join. He isn't old enough. He is six feet one inch, weighs 180, and won't be sixteen till the 5th of next February. Nobody ever saw him when he wasn't eating. They say he clips his words so as to save time for eating. He takes a cracker out of his pocket, shoves it in his mouth whole, jams his hat down till his ears stick out, and, with his companions, tears down the road, seemingly propelled as much by his elbows as by his legs. Why, under the combined strain of growing and running, he doesn't part a seam somewhere is a dark mystery.

Crash! The roof of the barn caves in and reveals what we had not before suspected, that Platt's barn, on the other side of the alley, is afire too. Say! This is getting interesting. The wind is setting directly toward Swope's house. It has been so terribly dry this last month or so that the house will go like powder if it ever catches. Why, I think Swope has a well and cistern both. Used to have, anyway, before they put the water-works in, and the board of health condemned the wells. Say! There was a put-up job if there ever was one. Why, sure! Sure he had stock in the water works. Doc. Muzzey? I guess, yes . . . . Pity they ever traded off the hand-engine. They got a light-running hook-and-ladder truck. Won two prizes at the tournament, just with that truck. But if they had that hand-engine now though! "Up with her! Down with her!" Have that fire out in no time!

They're not trying to save the barns. They're a dead loss. What little water they can get from the cisterns and wells around - hasn't it been dry? - they are using to try to save Swope's house, and the one next to it. Is that where Lonny Wheeler lives? I knew it was up this way somewhere. Don't he look ridiculous, sitting up there a-straddle of his ridgepole, with a tin-cup? A tin-cup, if you please. Over this way a little. See better.

They're wetting down the roof. Line of fellows passing buckets to the ladder, and a line up the ladder. What big sparks those are! Puts you in mind of Fourth of July. How the roof steams! Must be hot up there.

O-o-o-oh!

A universal indrawn breath from all spectators proclaims their horror. One of the men on the roof missed his footing and slipped, rolling over and over till he reached the roof of the porch, where he spread-eagled for a fall. The women begin to moan. Some poor fellow gone to his death. Or, if he be so lucky as to miss death itself, he is doomed to languish all his days a helpless cripple. Like enough the sole support of an aged mother; or perhaps his wife is sitting up for him at home now, tiptoeing into the bedroom every little while to look at the sleeping children. That's generally the way of it. Who is there so free and foot-loose that, if harm befall him, some woman will not go mourning all her days? It must take the heart out of brave men to think what their women folk must suffer, mothers and wives and - Who? Dan O'Brien? Oh, he'll be all right. He'll light on his feet like a cat. I believe that boy is made of India rubber. He never gets hurt. Why, one time - Ah! There he goes now up the ladder as if nothing had happened. Hooray-ayayay! Hooray-ay-ay-ay! I thought he'd broken his neck as sure as shooting.

Wandering about one cannot fail to encounter what the gallant fire-laddies have rescued from the devouring element. There is the piano with a deep scratch across the upper part, and the top lid hanging by one hinge. It caught in the door, and the boys were kind of in a hurry. There is the parlor carpet, plucked up by the roots, as it were; and two tubs, the washboard and a bag of clothes-pins; a stuffed chair, with three casters gone, the coffee-pot, a crayon enlargement, a winter overcoat, a blanket, a pile of old dresses, the screwdriver and a paper of tacks in the colander, the couch with a triangular rip in the cover, the coal-scuttle, a pile of dishes, the ax and wood-saw, a fancy pillow, the sewing-machine with the top gone, the wash-boiler, the basket of dirty clothes, with the stove-shaker and the parlor clock in together, and a heap of books, all spraddled and sprawled every which way. Upon this pitiful mound sits Mrs. Swope with her baby sound asleep upon her bosom. She mingles her tears with the sustaining tea that Mrs. Farley has made for her. Swope, still in his socks and with his wife's shoulder-cape upon him, caught up somehow, is trying to soothe her. He is as mad as a hornet, and doesn't dare to show it. All this furniture he had insured. It was all old stuff their folks had given them. If the gallant fire-laddies had been as discreet as they were zealous, they would have let the furniture go, and Swope and his wife would have had an entire, brand-new outfit. As it is, who can ever make that junk look like anything any more?

What's this coming up the road? Jumbo Lee and his friends with the other hose-reel. Now they will connect it with the hydrant, and have water a-plenty to save the house. Now the fellows are coming down from the ladder. Cistern's empty, I suppose. The other reel didn't come any too soon. How the roof steams! Or is it smoking?

"Don't stand around here with that reel! Up to that water-plug. Farther up the street. Front o' Cummins's."

Jumbo crams another cracker into his mouth and speeds away, hunching the patient, unresenting air with his elbows.

Ah! See - that little flicker of flame on the roof! Do, for pity's sake, hurry up with that connection! The roof is really burning. See? They are trying to chop away the burning place. But there's another! And another!

A-a-ah! Hooray-ay! Connection's made! Now you'll see something. Out of the way there! One side! One side! Up you go! . . . Wha-at? Is that the best they can do? Why, it won't run out of the nozzle at all when it's up on the roof. Not a drop. Feeble little dribble when it's on the ground-level. There's your water-works for you. It is a good long way from the fire-plug I know, but there ought to be more pressure than that. Oh, pshaw! If we only had the old hand-engine! "Up with her! Down with her!" Have that fire out in no time. The house will have to go now. Too bad!

Somebody in the second story is rescuing property from the devouring element. He has just tossed out a wash-bowl and pitcher. Luckily they both fell on the sod and rolled apart. He takes down the roller-shade and flings it out. The lace curtains follow. They catch on the edge of the veranda roof, and languidly wave there as for some holiday. Bed-clothes issue and pillows hurtle out. What's he doing now? No use. No use. You can't get the mattress out of that window. A waste-paper basket, a rag rug, a brush and comb - as fast as his hands can fly he's throwing out things.

The women began to whimper.

"Oh, the poor man! The roof will fall in on him! He'll

smother to death! Oh, why doesn't somebody go tell him to come away? Not you! Don't you think of such a trick! Oh, why does he risk his life for a lot of trash I wouldn't have around the house?"

The smoke oozes out of the open window. It must be choking in there. For a long time no jettison of household goods appears. Perhaps the man, whoever he is, has seen his peril and fled while yet it was possible to flee. Ah, but suppose he has been overcome and lies there huddled in a heap, never to rouse again? Is there none to save him? Is there none? Ah! A couple of collars and a magazine flutter out into the light! He is still there. He is still alive. Plague take the idiot! Why doesn't he come down out of that?

"Yoffemoffemoffemoffemoff. Yoffemoff!"

But no! He will do it himself. The Chief rushes gallantly into the burning building and disappears up the dark stair.

Desperate measures are now to be resorted to. On the lawn a line of men forms. They bend their necks, cowering before the fierce glow, but daring it, and prepared to face it at even closer range. You are to witness now an exhibition of that heroism which is commoner with us than we think, that spirit of do and dare which mocks at danger and even welcomes pain. It is a far finer sentiment than the cold-hearted calculation which looks ahead, and figures out first whether it is worth while or not.

The men dash forward in the withering heat. With frantic haste they fix the hook into the lattice-work beneath the porch and scamper back.

"Yo hee! Yo hee!"

The thick rope tautens as the firemen lay their weight to it. You can almost see the bristling fibers stand up on it.

"Yo hee! Yo hee!"

With a splintering crash the timber parts, and a piece of lattice-work is dragged away.

Another sortie and another. Bit by bit the porch is ripped and torn to rubbish. You smile. It seems so futile. What are these kindlings saved when the whole house is burning? Is this what you call heroism? Yet the charge at Balaklava was not more futile. It had even less of commonsense, less of hope of benefit to mankind to back it and inspire it. Heroism is an instinct, not a thoughtout policy. Its quality is the same, in two-ounce samples or in car-load lots.

The weather-boarding slips down in a sparkling fall. The joists and stringers, all outlined and gemmed with coals, are, as it were, a golden grille, through which the world may look unhindered in upon the holy place of home, heretofore conventually private. There stands the family altar, pitifully grotesque amid the ruinous splendor of the destroying fire, the tea-kettle upon it proudly flaunting its steamy plume. What? Is a common cooking-stove an altar? Yes, verily, in lineal descent. Examine an ancient altar and you will see its sacrificial stone scored and guttered to catch the dripping from the roasting meat. Who is the priestess, after an order older than Melchisedec's, but she that ministers to us that most comfortable sacrament, wherein we are made partakers not alone of the outward and visible food which we do carnally press with our teeth, but also of that inward and spiritual sustenance, the patient and enduring love of wife and mother, without which there can be no such thing as home? All other sacraments wherein men break the bread of amity together are but copies of this pattern, the Blessed Sacrament of the Household Altar, the first and primal one of all, the one that shall perdure, please God! throughout all ages of ages.

The flames die down. The timbers sink together with a softer fall. The air grows chill. We fetch a sigh. We cannot bear to look at that mute figure of the priestess seated on the sordid heap of broken furniture, her sleeping baby pressed against her breast, her gaze fixed - but seeing naught - upon her ruined temple. We do not like to think upon such things. We do not like to think at all. Is there nothing more to laugh at?

The firemen, having all borrowed the makings of a cigarette from each other, put on their hats and coats, left on the hook-and-ladder truck in the custody of a trusted member. The apparatus trundles off, the bells dolorously tolling as the striking gear on the rear axle engages the cam.

Who is this weeping man approaches, supported by two friends, that comfort him with: "All right, Tom. You done noble," uttered in pacifying if not convincing tones? Heart-brokenly he cries: "I dull le ver' bes' I knowed, now di' n't I? Charley? Billy, I dub bes' I knowed how. An' nen he says to me - Oo-hoo-hoo-oooo-oo! He says to me: 'Come ou' that, ye cussed fool!' Oo-oooo-hoo-hoo-oo-oo! Smf! Lemme gi' amma ham hankshiff. Leg go my arm. Waw gi' amma hankshifp. Oo-oo-oo-hoo-hoo-oo-oo! Fmf! I ash you as may wurl - I ash you as may - man of world, is that - is that proper way address me? Me! Know who I am? I'm Tom Ball. 'S who I am. I kill lick em man ill Logan Coun'y. Ai' thasso? Hay? 'S aw ri. Mfi choose stay up there, aw thas sec - aw thas second floor and rescue fel-cizzen's propprop'ty from devouring em - from devouring emlement, thas my bizless. Ai' tham my bizless, Charley? Ai' tham my bizless, Billy? W'y, sure. Charley, you're goof feller. You too, Billy. You're goof feller, too. Say. Wur-wur if Miller's is open yet? 'Spose it is? Charley; I dub bes' I knowed how, di'n't I, now? Affor that Chief come up thas stairway and say me: 'Come ou' that, ye cussed fool!' Aw say! 'Come ou' that - 'Called me fool, too! Oo-hoo-hoo-oo-oo-oo!"

"Hello, Dan! Hurt yourself any? (That's Dan O'Brien. Fell off the roof.) Well, sir, I thought sure you'd broken your neck. You don't know your luck. And let me tell you one thing, my bold bucko: You'll do that just once too often. Now you mark."

The day before the Weekly Examiner goes to press, Mr. Swope hands the editor a composition entitled: "A Card of Thanks," signed by John K. and Amelia M. Swope, and addressed to the firemen and all who showed by their many acts of kindness, and so forth and so on.

"Kind of help to fill up the paper," says Mr. Swope, covering his retreat.

"Sure," replies the editor. When Mr. Swope is good and gone, he says: "Dog my riggin's if I didn't forget all about writing up that fire. Been so busy here lately. Good thing he come in. Hay, Andy!"

"Watch want?" from the composing-room.

"Got room for about two sticks more?"

"Yes, guess so. If it don't run over that."

A brief silence. Then:

"Hay, Andy?"

"What ?"

"Is it 'had have,' or 'had of ?"

"What's the connection?"

"Why-ah. 'If the gallant fire-laddies, under the able direction of Chief Charley Lomax, had of had a sufficiency of water with which to cope with the devouring element - 'etc."

"'Had have,' I guess. I don't know."

"Guess you're right. Run it that way anyhow."

CIRCUS DAY

Only the other day, the man that in all this country knows better than anybody else how a circus should be advertised, said (with some sadness, I do believe) that it didn't pay any longer to put up showbills; the money was better invested in newspaper advertising.

"It doesn't pay." Ah, me! How the commercial spirit of the age plays whaley with the romance of existence! You shall not look. long upon the showbill now that there is no money to be had from it. "Youth's sweet-scented manuscript" is about to close, but ere it does, let us turn back a little to the pages illuminated by the glowing colors of the circus poster.

Saturday afternoon when we went by the enginehouse, its brick wall fluttered with the rags and tatters of "Esther, the Beautiful Queen," and the lecture on "The Republic: Will it Endure?" (Gee! But that was exciting!) Sunday morning, after Sunday-school, there was a sudden quickening among the boys. We stopped nibbling on the edges of the lesson leaf and followed the crowd in scuttling haste. Miraculously, over-night, the shabby wall had blossomed into thralling splendor. What was Daniel in the Lions' Den, compared with Herr Alexander in the same? Not, as the prophet is pictured, in the farthest corner from the lions, and manifestly saying to himself: "If I was only out of this!" But with his head right smack dab in the lion's mouth. Right in it. Yes, sir.

"S' Posin'!" we gasped, all goggle-eyed, "jist s'posin' that there lion was to shut his mouth! Ga-ash!"

The Golden Text? It faded before the lemon-and-scarlet glories of the Golden Chariot. Drawn by sixteen dappled steeds, each with his neck arching like a fish-hook and reined with fancy scalloped reins, it occupied the center of the foreground. The band rode in it, far more fortunate than our local band whose best was, Charley Wells's depot 'bus. And nobler than all his fellows was the bass-drummer. He had a canopy over him, a carved and golden canopy, on whose top revolved a clown's head with its tongue stuck out. On each quarter of this rococo shallop a golden circus-girl in short skirts gaily skipped rope with a nubia or fascinator, or whatever it is the women call the thing they wrap around their heads in cold weather when they hang out the clothes. There were big pieces of looking-glass let into the sides of the band-wagon, and every decorator knows that when you put looking-glass on a thing it is impossible to fix it so that it will be any finer.

Winding back and forth across the picture was the long train of tableau-cars and animal cages, diminishing with distance until away, 'way up in the upper left-hand corner the hindmost van was all immersed in the blue-and-yellow haze just this side of out-of-sight. That with our own eyes we should behold the glories here set forth we knew right well. Cruel Fortune might cheat us of the raptures to be had inside the tents, but the street-parade was ours, for it was free.

It seems to me that we did not linger so long before these pictures, nor before those of the rare and costly animals, which, if we but knew it, were the main reason why we were permitted to go (if we did get to go). To look at these animals is improving to the mind, and since we could not go alone, an older person had to accompany us, and . . . and . . . I trust I make myself clear. But we didn't want to improve our minds if it was a possible thing to avoid it. The pictures of these animals were in the joggerfy book anyhow, though not in colors, unless we had a box of paints. There can be no doubt that the show-bill pictures of the menageries were in colors. I seem to recollect that Mr. Galbraith, who kept the dry-goods store across the street from the engine-house, was very much exercised in his mind about the way one of these pictures was printed. It was the counterfeit presentment of the Hip-po-pot-a-mus, or Behemoth of Holy Writ. His objection to the hip - you know was not because its open countenance was so fearsome, but because it was so red. Six feet by two of flaming crimson across the street in the afternoon sun made it necessary for him to take the goods to the back window of the store to show to customers. He didn't like it a bit.

No. Neither before the large and expensive pictures of the street-parade, nor the large and expensive wild beasts did we linger. The swarm was thickest, sand the jabbering loudest, the "O-o-oh's," the "M! Looky's" the "Geeminently's" shrillest, in front of where the deeds of high emprise were set forth. Men with their fists clenched on their breasts, and their neatly slippered toes touching the backs of their heads, crashed through paper-covered hoops beneath which horses madly coursed; they flew through the air with the greatest of ease, the daring young men on the flying; trapeze, or they posed in living pyramids.

And as the sons of men assembled themselves together, Satan came also, the spirit I, that evermore denies.

"A-a-ah!" sneers his embodiment in one whose crackling voice cannot make up its mind whether to be bass or treble, "A-a-ah, to the show they down't do hay-uf what they is in the pitchers."

A chilling silence follows. A cold uneasiness strikes into all the listeners. We are all made wretched by destructive criticism. Let us alone in our ideals. Let us alone, can't you?

"Now . . . now," pursues the crackle-voiced Mephisto, pointing to where Japanese jugglers defy the law of gravitation and other experiences of daily life, "now, they cain't walk up no ladder made out o' reel sharp swords."

"They can so walk up it," stoutly declares one boy. Hurrah! A champion to the rescue! The others edge closer to him. They like him.

"Nah, they cain't. How kin they? They'd cut their feet all to pieces."

"They kin so. I seen 'em do it. The time I went with Uncle George I seen a man, a Japanee . . . . Yes, sharp. Cut paper with 'em. . . . A-a-ah, I did so. I guess I know what I seen an' what I didn't."

The little boys breathe easier, but fearing another onslaught, make all haste to call attention to the most fascinating one of all, the picture of a little boy standing up on top of his daddy's head. And, as if that weren't enough, his daddy is standing up on a horse and the horse is going round the ring lickety-split. And, as if these circumstances weren't sufficiently trying, that little show-boy is standing on only one foot. The other is stuck up in the air like five minutes to six, and he has hold of his toe with his hand. I'll bet you can't do that just as you are on the ground, let alone on your daddy's head, and him on a horse that's going like sixty. Now you just try it once. Just try it. . . . Aa-ah! Told you you couldn't.

Now, how the show-actors can do that looks very wonderful to you. It really is very simple. I'll tell you about it. All show-actors are born double-jointed. You have only two hip-joints. They have four. And it's the same all over with them. Where you have only one joint, they have two. So, you see, the wonder isn't how they can bend themselves every which way, but how they can keep from doubling up like a foot-rule.

And another thing. Every day they rub themselves all over with snake-oil. Snakes are all limber and supple, and it stands to reason that if you take and try out their oil, which is their express essence, and then rub that into your skin, it will make you supple and limber, too. I should think garter-snakes would do all right, if you could catch enough of them, but they 're so awfully scarce. Fishworms won't do. I tried 'em. There's no grease in 'em at all. They just dry up.

And I suppose you know the reason why they stay on the horse's back. They have rosin on their feet. Did you ever stand up on a horse's back? I did. It was out to grandpap's, on old Tib. . . .No, not very long. I didn't have any rosin on my feet. I was going to put some on, but my Uncle Jimmy said: "Hay! What you got there?" I told him. "Well," he says, "you jist mosey right into the house and put that back in the fiddle-box where you got it. Go on, now. And if I catch you foolin' with my things again, I'll . . . . Well, I don't know what I will do to you." So I put it back. Anyhow, I don't think rosin would have helped me stay on a second longer, because old Tib, with an intelligence you wouldn't have suspected in her, walked under the wagon-shed and calmly scraped me off her back.

And did you ever try to walk the tight-rope? You take the clothes-line and stretch it in the grape-arbor - better not make it too high at first - and then you take the clothes-prop for a balance-pole and go right ahead - er - er as far as you can. The real reason why you fall off so is that you don't have chalk on your shoes. Got to have lots of chalk. Then after you get used to the rope wabbling so all-fired fast, you can do it like a mice. And while I'm about it, I might as well tell you that if you ever expect to amount to a hill of beans as a trapeze performer you must have clear-starch with oil of cloves in it to rub on your hands. Finest thing in the world. My mother wouldn't let me have any. She said she couldn't have me messing around that way, I blame her as much as anybody that I am not now a competent performer on the trapeze.

I don't know that I had better go into details about the state of mind boys are in from the time the bills are first put up until after the circus has actually departed. I don't mean the boys that get to go to everything that comes along, and that have pennies to spend for candy, and all like that, whenever they ask for it. I mean the regular, proper, natural boys, that used to be "Back

Home," boys whose daddies tormented them with: "Well, we ll see - " that's so exasperating! - or, "I wish you wouldn't tease, when you know we can't spare the money just at present." A perfectly foolish answer, that last. They had money to fritter away at the grocery, and the butcher-shop, and the dry-goods store, but when it came to a necessity of life, such as going to the circus, they let on they couldn't afford it. A likely story.

"Only jist this little bit of a once. Aw, now, please. Please, cain't I go? Aw now, I think you might. Aw now, woncha? Aw, paw. I ain't been to a reely show for ever so long. Aw, the Scripture pammerammer, that don't count. Aw, paw. Please cain't I go? Aw, please!" And so forth and so on, with much more of the same sort. No, I can't go into details. it's too terrible.

Even those of us whose daddies said plainly and positively: "Now, I can't let you go. No, Willie. That's the end of it. You can't go." Even those, I say, hoped against hope. It simply could not be that what the human heart so ardently longed for should be denied by a loving father. This same conviction applies to other things, even when we are grown up. It is against nature and the constituted scheme of things that we cannot have what we want so badly. (And, in general, it may be said that we can have almost anything we want, if we only want it hard enough. That's the trouble with us. We don't want it hard enough.) We boys lay there in the shade and pulled the long stalks of grass and nibbled off the sweet, yellow ends, as we dramatized miracles that could happen just as well as not, if they only would, consarn 'em! For instance, you might be going along the street, not thinking of anything but how much you wanted to go to the circus, and how sorry you were because you hadn't the money, and your daddy wouldn't give you any; and first thing you 'd know, you 'd stub your toe on something, and you'd look down and there'd be a half a dollar that somebody had lost - Gee! If it would only be that way! But we knew it wouldn't, because only the other Sunday, Brother Longenecker had said: "The age of miracles is past." So we had to give up all hopes. Oh, it's terrible. Just terrible!

But some of the boys lay there in the grass with their hands under their heads, looking up at the sky, and making little white spots come in and out on the corners of their jaws, they had their teeth set so hard, and were chewing so fiercely. You could almost hear their minds creak, scheming, scheming, scheming. I suppose there were ways for boys to make money in those times, but they always fizzled out when you came to try them, to say nothing of the way they broke into your day. Why, you had scarcely any time to play in. You 'd go 'round to some neighbor's house with a magazine, and you'd say: "Good afternoon, Mrs. Slaymaker. Do you want to subscribe for this?" Just the way you had studied out you would say. And she'd take it, and go sit down with it, and read it clear through while you played with the dog, and then when she got all through with it, and had read all the advertisements, she'd hand it back to you and say: No, she didn't believe she would. They had so many books and papers now that she didn't get a chance hardly to read in any of them, let alone taking any new ornes. Were you getting many new subscribers? Just commenced, eh? Well, she wished you all the luck in the world. How was your ma? That's good. Did she hear from your Uncle John's folks since they moved out to Kansas?

I have heard that there were boys who, under the dire necessity of going to the circus, got together enough rags, old iron, and bottles to make up the price, sold 'em, collected the money, and went. I don't believe it. I don't believe it. We all had, hidden under the back porch, our treasure-heap of rusty grates, cracked fire-pots, broken griddles and lid-lifters, tub-hoops and pokers, but I do not believe that any human boy ever collected fifty cents' worth. I want you to understand that fifty cents is a whole lot of money, particularly when it is laid out in scrap-iron. Only the tin-wagon takes rags, and they pay in tinware, and that's no good to a boy that wants to go to the circus. And as for bottles - well, sir, you wash out a whole, whole lot of bottles, a whole big lot of 'em, a wash-basket full, and tote 'em down to Mr. Case's drug - and book-store, as much as ever you and your brother can wag, and see what he gives you. It's simply scandalous. You have no idea of how mean and stingy a man can be until you try to sell him old bottles. And the cold-hearted way in which he will throw back ink-bottles that you worked so hard to clean, and the ones that have reading blown into the glass - Oh, it's enough to set you against business transactions all your life long. There's something about bargain and sale that's mean and censorious, finding this fault and finding that fault, and paying just as little as ever they can. It gets on one's nerves. It really does.

The boys that made the little white spots come on the corners of their jaws as they lay there in the grass, scheming, scheming, scheming, planned rags, and bottles, and scrap-iron, and more also. Sometimes it was a plan so much bigger that if they had kept it to themselves, like the darkey's cow, they would have "all swole up and died."

"Sst! Come here once. Tell you sumpum. Now don't you go and blab it out, now will you? Hope to die? Well . . . . Now, no kiddin'. Cross your heart? Well . . . Ah, you will, too. I know you. You go and tattle everything you hear . . . . Well. . . . Cheese it! Here comes somebody. Make out we're talkin' about sumpum else. Ah, he did, did he? What for, I wonder? (Say sumpum, can't ye?) Why 'nu' ye say sumpum when he was goin' by? Now he'll suspicion sumpum 's up, and nose around till he . . . . Aw, they ain't no use tellin' you anything . . . . Well. Put your head over so 's I can whisper. Sure I am. . . . Well, I could learn, couldn't I? Now don't you tell a living soul, will you? If anybody asts you, you tell 'em you don't know anything at all about it. Say, why 'n't you come along? I promised you the last time. That's jist your mother callin' you. Let on you don't hear her. Aw, stay. Aw, you don't either have to go. Say. Less you and me get up early, and go see the circus come in town, will you? I will, if you will. All right. Remember now. Don't you tell anybody what I told you. You know."

If a fellow just only could run off with a circus! Wouldn't it be great? No more splitting kindling and carrying in coal; no more: "Hurry up, now, or you'll be late for school;" no more poking along in a humdrum existence, never going any place or seeing anything, but the glad, free, untrammeled life, the life of a circus-boy, standing up on top of somebody's head (you could pretend he was your daddy. Who'd ever know the difference?) and your leg stuck up like five minutes to six, and him standing on top of a horse - and the horse going around the ring, and the ring master cracking his whip - aw, say! How about it?

Maybe the show-people would take you even if you

didn't have two joints to common folks' one, and hadn't had early advantages in the way of plenty of snakes to try the grease out of. And then . . .and then. . . . Travel all around, and be in a new town every day! And see things! The water-works, and Main Street, and the Soldiers' Monument, and the Second Presbyterian Church. All the sights there are to see in strange places. And then when the show came back to your own home-town next year, people would wonder whose was that slim and gracile figure in the green silk tights and spangled breech-clout that capered so nimbly on the bounding courser's back, that switched the natty switch and shrilly called out: "Hep! Hep!" They'd screw up their eyes to look hard, and they'd say: "Yes, sir. It is. It's him. It's Willie Bigelow. Well, of all things!" And they'd clap their hands, and be so proud of you. And they'd wonder how it was that they could have been so blind to your many merits when they had you with them. They'd feel sorry that they ever said you were a "regular little imp," if ever there was one, and that you had the Old Boy in you as big as a horse. They'd feel ashamed of themselves, so they would. And they'd come and apologize to you for the way they had acted, and you'd say: "Oh, that's all right. Forgive and forget." And they'd miss you at home, too. Your daddy would wish he hadn't whaled you the way he did, just for nothing at all. And your mother, too, she'd be sorry for the way she acted to you, tormenting the life and soul out of you, sending you on errands just when you got a man in the king row, and making you wash your feet in a bucket before you went to bed, instead of being satisfied to let you pump on them, as any reasonable mother would. She'll think about that when you're gone. It'll be lonesome then, with nobody to bang the doors, and upset the cream-pitcher on the clean table-cloth, and fall over backward in the rocking-chair and break a rocker off. Your daddy will sigh and say:

"I wonder where Willie is to-night. Poor boy, I sometimes fear I was too harsh with him." And your mother will try to keep back her tears, but she can't, and first thing she knows she'll burst out crying, and . . and . . . and old Maje will go around the house looking for you, and whining because he can't find his little playmate . . . . It will seem as if you were dead - dead to them, and . . . . Smf! Smf!

(Confound that orchestra leader anyhow! How many times have I got to tell him that this is the music-cue for "Where is My Wandering Boy To-night?")

We were all going to get up early enough to see the show come in at the depot. Very few of us did it. Somehow we couldn't seem to wake up. Here and there a hardy spirit compasses the feat.

All the town is asleep when this boy slips out of his front-gate and snicks the latch behind him softly. It is very still, so still that though he is more than a mile away from the railroad he can hear Johnny Mara, the night yardmaster, bawl out: "Run them three empties over on Number Four track!" the short exhaust of the obedient pony-engine, and the succeeding crash of the cars as they bump against their fellows. It is very still, scarey still. The gas-lamp flaring and flickering among the green maples at the corner has a strange look to him. His footfalls on the sidewalk sound so loud he takes the soft middle of the dusty road. He hears some one pursuing him and his bosom contracts with fear, as he stands to see who it is. Although he hardly knows the boy bound on the same errand as his, he takes him to his heart, as a chosen friend. They are kin.

On the freight-house platform they find other boys. Some of them have waited up all night so as not to miss it. They are from across the tracks. They have all the fun, those fellows do. They can swear and chew tobacco, and play hookey from school and have a good time. They get to go barefoot before anybody else, and nobody tells them it will thin their blood to go in swimming so much. Yes, and they can fight, too. They'd sooner fight than eat. Our boys, conscious of inferiority, keep to themselves. The boys from across the tracks show off all the bad words they can think of. One of them has a mouth-harp which he plays upon, now and then opening his hands hollowed around the instrument. Patsy Gubbins dances to the music, which is a thing even more reckless and daredevil than swearing. Patsy's going with a "troupe" some day. Or else, he's going to get a job firing on an engine. He isn't right sure which he wants to do the most.

Now and then a brakeman goes by swinging his lantern. The boys would like to ask him what time it is, but for one thing they're too bashful. Being a brakeman is almost as good as going with a "troupe" or a circus. You get to go to places that way, too, Marysville, and Mechanicsburg, and Harrod's - that is, if you're on the local freight, and then you lay over in Cincinnati. Some ways it's better than firing, and some ways it isn't so good. And then there is another reason why they don't ask the brakeman what time it is. He'd say it was "forty-five" or maybe "fifty-three," and never tell what hour.

"Say! Do you know it's cold? You wouldn't think it would be so cold in the summer-time."

The maple-trees, from being formless blobs, insensibly begin to look like lace-work. Presently the heavens and the earth are bathed in liquid blue that casts a spell so potent on the soul of him that sees it that he yearns for something he knows not what, except that it is utterly beyond him, as far beyond him as what he means to be will be from what he shall attain to. One dreams of romance and renown, of all that should be and is not. And as he dreams the birds awaken. In the East there comes a greenish tinge. Far up the track, there is a sullen roar, and then the hoarse diapason of an engine whistle. The roar strengthens and strengthens. It is the circus train.

Under the witchcraft of the dreaming blue, each boy had a firm and stubborn purpose. Over and over again he rehearsed how he would go up to the man that runs the show, and say: "Please, mister, can I go with you?" And the man would say, "Yes." (As easy as that.) But the purpose wavered as he saw the roustabouts come tumbling out, all frowsy and unwashed, rubbing the sleep out of their eyes, cross and savage. And the man whose word they jump to obey, he's kind of discouraging. it's all business with him. The fellows may plead with their eyes; he never sees them. If he does, he tells them where to get to out of that and how quick he wants it done, in language that makes the boldest efforts of the boys from across the tracks seem puny in comparison. The lads divide into two parties. One follows the buggy of the boss canvasman to Vandeman's lots where the stand is made. They will witness the spectacle of the raising of the tents, but they will also be near the man that runs the show, and if all goes well it may be he will like your looks and saunter up to you and say: "Well, bub, and how would you like to travel with us?" You don't know. Things not half so strange as that have happened. And if you were right there at the time . . . .

The other party lingers awhile looking up wistfully at the unresponsive windows of the sleeping-cars, behind which are the happy circus-actors. Perhaps the show-boy that stands up on top of his daddy's head will look out. If he should raise the window and smile at you, and get to talking with you maybe he would introduce you to his pa, and tell him that you would like to go with the show, and his pa would be a nice sort of a man, and he'd say: "Why, yes. I guess we can fix that all right." And there you'd be.

Or if it didn't come out like that, why, maybe the boy would be another "Little Arthur, the Boy Circus-rider," like it told about in he Ladies' Repository. It seems there was a man, and one day he went by where there was a circus, and in a quiet secluded, vine-clad nook only a few steps from the main tent, he heard somebody sigh, oh, so sadly and so pitifully! Come to find out, it was Little Arthur, the Boy Circus-rider. He had large sensitive violet eyes, and a wealth of clustering ringlets, and he was very, very unhappy. So the man took from his pocket a Bible that he happened to have with him, and he read from it to Little Arthur, which cheered him up right away, because up to that moment he had only heard of the Bible. (Think of that!) And that night at the show, what do you s'pose? Little Arthur fell off the horse and hurt himself. And this man was at the show and he went back in the dressing-room, and held Little Arthur's hand. And the clown was crying, and the actors were crying, for they all loved Little Arthur in their rude, untutored way. And Little Arthur opened his large sensitive violet eyes, and saw the man, and said off the text that the man taught him that afternoon.

And then he died. It was a sad story, but it made you wish it had been you that happened to have a Bible in your pocket as you passed the secluded, vine-clad nook only a few paces from the main tent, and had heard Little Arthur sigh so pitifully. It was those sensitive eyes we looked for in the sleeping-car windows, and all in vain. I think I saw the wealth of clustering ringlets, or at least the makings of it. I am almost positive I saw curl-papers as the curtain was drawn aside a moment.

But whether a boy stands gazing at the sleepers, or runs over to the lots, there is something pathetic about it, something almost terrible. It is the death of an ideal. I can't conceive of a boy coming down to the depot to see the circus train come in another time. Hitherto, the show has been to him the ne plus ultra of romance. It comes in the night from 'way off yonder; it goes in the night to 'way off yonder. It is all splendor, all deeds of high emprise. It stands to reason then, that the closer you get to it, the closer you get to pure romance. And it isn't that way at all.

What gravels a boy the most of all is to have to do the same old thing over and over again, day after day, week in, week out. Once he has seen the circus come in, he cannot blind himself to the fact that everything is marked and numbered; that all is system, and that everything is done today exactly as it was done yesterday, and as it will be done tomorrow.

"What town is this?" he hears a man inquire of another.

"Blest if I know. What's the odds what town it is?"

Didn't know what town it was! Didn't care!

The keen morning air, or something, makes a fellow mighty unromantic, too. Perhaps it was the thin blue wood-smoke from the field-stoves, and the smell of the hot coffee and the victuals the waiters are carrying about, some to the tent where the bare tables are for the canvasmen, some to the table covered with a red and white table-cloth as befits performers. These have no rosy cheeks. Their lithe limbs are not richly decked with silken tights. Insensibly the upper lip curls. They're not so much. They're only folks. That's all, just folks.

But when ideals die, great truths are born. To such a boy at such a moment there comes the firm conviction which increasing years can only emphasize: Home is but a poor prosaic place, but Home - Ah, my brother, think on this - Home is where Breakfast is.

"Hay! Wait for me, you fellows! Hay! Hold on a minute. Well, ain't I a-comin' jis"s fast's ever I kin? What's your rush?"

It is the exceptional boy has this experience. The normal one preserves the delicate bloom of romance, by never seeing the show until it makes its Grand Triumphal Entree in a Pageant of Unparalleled Magnificence far Surpassing the Pomp and Splendor of Oriental Potentates.

The hitching-posts are full of whinnering country horses, and people are in town you wouldn't think existed if you hadn't seen their pictures in Puck and Yudge, people from over by Muchinippi, and out Noodletoozy way, big, red-necked men with the long loping step that comes from walking on the plowed ground. Following them are lanky women with their front teeth gone, and their figures bowed by drudgery, dragging wide-eyed children whose uncouth finery betrays the "country jake," even if the freckles and the sun-bleached hair could keep the secret. From the far-off fastnesses, where there are still log-cabins chinked with mud, they have ventured to see the show come into town, and when they have seen that, they will retire again beyond our ken. How every sense is numbed and stunned by the magnificence and splendor of the painted and gilded wagons as they rumble past, the driver rolling and pitching in his seat, as he handles the ribbons of eight horses all at once! The farmer's heart is filled with admiration of his craft, as much as the children's hearts are at the gaudy pictures.

The allegorical tableau-car solemnly waggles past, Europe, and Asia, and Africa, and Australia brilliant in grease-paint and gorgeous cheesecloth robes. And can you guess who the fat lady is up on the very tip-top of all, on the tip-top where the wobble is the worst? Our own Columbia! It must be fine to ride around that way all dressed up in a flag. But a sourer lot of faces you never saw in your life. No. I am wrong. For downright melancholy and despondency you must wait till the funny old clown comes along in his little bit of a buggy drawn by a little bit of a donkey.

"And, oh, looky! Here comes the elephants, just the same as in the joggerfy books. And see the men walking beside them. They come from the place the elephants do. See, they have on the clothes they wear in that country. Don't they look proud? Who wouldn't be proud to get to walk with an elephant? And if you ever do anything to an elephant to make him mad, he'll always remember it, and some day he'll get even with you. One time there was a man, and he gave an elephant a chew of tobacco, and - O-o-ooh! See that man in the cage with the lions! Don't it just make the cold chills run over you? I wouldn't be there for a million dollars, would you, ma?

"What they laughing at down the street? Ma, make Lizzie get down; she's right in my way. I don't want to see it pretty soon. I want to see it naow! Oh, ain't it funny? See the old clowns playing on horns! Ain't it too killing? Aw, look at them ponies. I woosht I had one. Johnny Pym has got a goat he can hitch up. What was that, pa? What was that went 'OoOOoohm!'"

"Whoa, Nell, whoa there! Steady, gal, steaday! Ho, there! Ho! Whoa -whoa-hup! Whad dy y' about? Fool horse. Whoa . . . whoa so, gal, soo-o. Lion, I guess, or a tagger, or sumpum or other."

And talk about music. You thought the band was grand. You just wait. Don't you hear it down the street? It'll be along in a minute now.

There it is. That's the cally-ope. That's what the show bills call: "The Steam Car of the Muses." . . . Mm-well, I don't know but it is just a leetle off the pitch, especially towards the end of a note, but you must remember that you can't haul a very big boiler on a wagon, and the whistles let out an awful lot of steam. It's pretty hard to keep the pressure even. But it's loud. That's the main thing. And the man that plays on it - no, not that fellow in the overalls with a wad of greasy waste in his hand. He 's only the engineer. I mean the artist, the man that plays on the keys. Well, he knows what the people want. He has his fingers on the public pulse. Does he give them a Bach fugue, or Guillmant's "Grand Choeur?" 'Deed, he doesn't. He goes right to the heart, with "Patrick's Day in the Morning," and "The Carnival of Venice," and "Home, Sweet Home," and "Oh, Where, Oh Where has my Little Dog Gone?" He knows his business. A shade off the key, perhaps, but my! Ain't it grand? So loud and nice!

"Well, that's all of it . . . . Why, child, I can't make it any longer than it is.

What do you want me to drive round into the other street for? You've seen all there is to see. Got all your trading done, mother? Well, then I expect we'd better put for home. Now, Eddy, I told you 'No' once, and that's the end of it. Hush up now! Look here, sir! Do you want me to take and 'tend to you right before everybody? Well, I will now, if I hear another whimper out o' ye. Ck-ck-ck! Git ep there, Nelly."

Some day, when we get big, and have whole, whole lots of money we're going to the circus every time it comes to town, to the real circus, the one you have to pay to get into. For if merely the street parade is so magnificent, what must the show itself be?

How people can sit at the table on circus day and stuff, and stuff the way they do is more than I can understand. You'd think they hadn't any more chances to eat than they had to go to the show. And they can find more things to do before they get started! And then, after the house is all locked up and everything, they've got to go back after a handkerchief! What does anybody want with a handkerchief at a circus?

It's exasperating enough to have to choose between

going in the afternoon and not going at all. Why, sure, it's finer at night. Lots finer. You know that kind of a light the peanut-roaster man has got down by the post-office. Burns that kind of stuff they use to take out grease-spots. Ye-ah. Gasoline. Well, at the circus at night, they don't have just one light like that, but bunches and bunches of them on the tentpoles. No, silly! Of course not. Of course they don't set the tent afire. But say! What if they did, eh? The place would be all full of people, laughing at the country jake that comes out to ride the trick-mule, and you'd happen to look up and see where the canvas was ju-u-ust beginning to blaze, and you'd jump up and holler: "Fire! Fire!" as loud as ever you could because you saw it first, and you'd point to the place. Excitement? Well, I guess yes. The people would all run every which way, and fall all over themselves, and the women would squeal - And do you know what I'd do? Wouldn't just let myself down between the kind of bedslat benches, and drop to the ground, and lift up the canvas and there I'd be all safe. And after I was all safe, then I'd go back and rescue folks.

We-ell, I s'pose I'd have to rescue a girl. It seems they always do that. But it would be nicer, I think, to rescue some real rich man. He'd say: "My noble preserver! How can I sufficiently reward you?" and take out his pocketbook. And wouldn't say: "Take back your proffered gold," and make like I was pushing it away, "take back your proffered gold. I but did my duty." And then wouldn't forget all about it. And one day, after I'd forgotten all about, it, the man would die, and will me a million dollars, or a thousand, I don't know. Enough to make me rich.

And say! Wouldn't the animals get excited when they

saw the show was afire? They'd just roar and roar, and upset the cages, and maybe they'd get loose. O-o-o-Oh! How about that? If there was a lion come at me I'd climb a tree. What would you do? Ah, your pa's shot-gun nothing! Why, you crazy, that would only infuriate him the more. What you want to do is to take an express rifle, like Doo Challoo did, and aim right for his heart. An express rifle is what you send off and get, and they ship it to you by express.

So you see what a fellow misses by having to go to the show in the afternoon, like the girls and the a-b-abs. The boys from across the tracks get to go at night. They have all the fun. When they go they don't have to poke along, and poke along, and keep hold of hands so as not to get lost. . . . Aw, hurry up, can't you? Don't you hear the band playing? It'll be all over before we get there.

But finally the lots are reached, and there are the tents, with all kinds of flags snapping from the centerpoles and the guy-ropes. And there are the sideshows. Alas! You never thought of the sideshows when you asked if you could go. And now it's too late. It must be fine in the side-shows. I never got to go to one. I didn't have the money. But if the big, painted banners, bulging in and out, as the wind plays with them, are anything to go by, it must be something grand to see the Fat Lady, and the Circassian Beauty, whose frizzled head will just about fit a bushel basket, and the Armless Wonder. They say he can take a pair of scissors with his toes and cut your picture out of paper just elegant.

Oh, and something else you miss by going in the afternoon. At night you can sneak around at the back, and when nobody is looking you can just lift up the canvas and go right in for nothing . . . . Why, what's wrong about that? Ah, you're too particular . . . . And if the canvasman catches you, you can commence to cry and say you had only forty cents, and wanted to see the circus so bad, and he'll take it and let you in, and you can have ten cents, don't you see, to spend for lemonade, red lemonade, you understand; and peanuts, the littlest bags, and the "on-riest" peanuts that ever were.

As far as I can see, the animal part of the show is just the same as it always was. The people that take you to the show always pretend to be interested in them, but it's my belief they stop and look only to tease you. Away, 'way back in ancient times, there used to be a man that took the folks around and told them what was in each cage, and where it came from, and how much it cost, and what useful purpose it served in the wise economy of nature, and all about it. That was before my time. But I can recollect something they had that they don't have any more. I can remember when Mr. Barnum first brought his show to our town. It didn't take much teasing to get to go to that, because in those days Mr. Barnum was a "biger man than old Grant." "The Life of P. T. Barnum, Written by Himself" was on everybody's marble-topped centertable, just the same as "The History of the Great Rebellion." You show some elderly person from out of town the church across the street from the Astor House, and say: "That's St. Paul's Chapel. General Montgomery's monument is in the chancel window. George Washington went to meeting there the day he was inaugurated president," and your friend will say: "M-hm." But you tell him that right across Broadway is where Barnum's Museum used to be, and he'll brighten right up and remember all about how Barnum strung a flag across to St. Paul's steeple and what a fuss the vestry of Trinity Parish made. That's something he knows about. that's part of the history of our country.

Well, when Mr. Barnum first came to our town, all around one tent were vans full of the very identical Moral Waxworks that we had read about, and had given up all hopes of ever seeing because New York was so far away. There was the Dying Zouave. Oh, that was a beauty! The Advance Courier said that "the crimson torrent of his heart's blood spouted in rhythmic jets as the tide of life ebbed silently away;" but I guess by the time they got to our town they must have run all out of pokeberry juice, for the "crimson torrent" didn't spout at all. But his bosom heaved every so often, and he rolled up his eyes something grand! I liked it, but my mother said it was horrid. That's the way with women. They don't like anything that anybody else does. There's no pleasing 'em. And she thought the Drunkard's Family was "kind o' low." It wasn't either. It was fine, and taught a great moral lesson. I told her so, but she said it was low, just the same. She thought the Temperance Family was nice, but it wasn't anywhere near as good as the Drunkard's Family. Why, let me tell you. The Drunkard's Wife was in a ragged calico dress, and her eye was all black and blue, where he had hit her the week before. And the Drunkard had hold of a black quart bottle, and his nose was all red, and he wore a plug hat that was even rustier and more caved in than Elder Drown's, if such a thing were possible. And there was - But I can't begin to tell you of all the fine things Mr. Barnum had that year, but never had again.

Another thing Mr. Barnum had that year that never appeared again. It may be that after that time the Funny

Old Clown did crack a joke, but I never heard him. The one that Mr. Barnum had got off the most comical thing you ever heard. I'll never forget it the longest day I live. Laugh? Why, I nearly took a conniption over it. It seems the clown got to crying about something . . . . Now what was it made him cry? Let me see now . . . . Ain't it queer I can't remember that? Fudge! Well, never mind now. It will come to me in a minute.

I feel kind of sorry for the poor little young ones that grow up and never know what a clown is like. Oh, yes, they have them to-day, after a fashion. They stub their toes and fall down the same as ever, but there is a whole mob of them and you can't take the interest in them that you could in "the one, the only, the inimitable" clown there used to be, a character of such importance that he got his name on the bills. He was a mighty man in those days. The ring-master was a kind of stuck-up fellow, very important in his own estimation, but he didn't have a spark of humor. Not a spark. And he'd be swelling around there, all so grand, and the clown, just to take him down a peg or two, would ask him a conundrum. And do you think he could ever guess one? Never. Not a one. And when the clown would tell him what the answer was, he'd be so vexed at himself that he'd try to take it out on the poor clown, and cut at him with his long whip. But Mr. Clown was just as spry in his shoes as he was under the hat, and he'd hop up on the ring-side out of the way, and squall out: "A-a-aah! Never touched me!" We had that for a byword. Oh, you'd die laughing at the comical remarks he'd make. And he'd be so quick about it. The ring-master would say something, and before you'd think, the clown would make a joke out of it . . . . I wish I could remember what it was he said that was so funny, the time he started crying. Seems to me it was something about his little brother . . . . Well, no matter.

Yes, sir, there are heads of families to-day, I'll bet you, that have grown up without ever having heard a clown sing a comic song, and ask the audience to join in the chorus. And if you say to such people: "Here we are again, Mr. Merryman," or "Bring on another horse," or "What will the little lady have now? the banners, my lord?" they look at you so funny. They don't know what you mean, and they don't know whether to get huffy or not. Well, I suppose it had to be that the Funny Old Clown with all his songs, and quips, and conundrums, and comical remarks should disappear. Perhaps he "didn't pay."

I can't see that the rest of the show has changed so very much. Perhaps the trapeze performances are more marvelous and breath-suspending than they used to be. But they were far and far beyond what we could dream of then, and to go still farther as little impresses us as to be told that people live still even westerly of Idaho. The trapeze performers are up-to-date in one respect. The fellow that comes down with his arms folded, one leg stuck out and the other twined around the big rope, revolving slowly, slowly - well, the band plays the Intermezzo from "Cavalleria Rusticana" nowadays when he does that. It used to play: "O Thou, Sweet Spirit, Hear my Prayer!" But the lady in the riding-habit still smiles as if it hurt her when her horse walks on its hind legs; the bareback rider does the very same fancy steps as the horse goes round the ring in a rocking-chair lope; the attendants still slant the hurdles almost flat for the horse to jump; they still snake the banners under the rider's feet as he gives a little hop up, and they still bang him on the head with the paper-covered hoop to . . . . Hold on a minute. Now.

Now . . . That story the clown told that was so funny, that had something to do with those hoops. I wish I could think of it. It would make you laugh, I know.

People try to lay the blame of the modern circus's failure to interest them on the three rings. They say so many things to watch at once keeps them from being watching properly any one act. They can't give it the attention it deserves. But I'll tell you what's wrong: There isn't any Funny Old Clown, a particular one, to give it human interest. It is all too splendid, too magnificent, too far beyond us. We want to hear somebody talk once in awhile.

They pretended that the tent was too big for the clown to be heard, but I take notice it wasn't too big for the fellow to get up and declaim "The puffawmance ees not yait hawf ovah. The jaintlemanly agents will now pawss around the ring with tickets faw the concert." I used to hate that man. When he said the performance was not yet half over, he lied like a dog, consarn his picture! There were only a few more acts to come. He knew it and we knew it. We wanted the show to go on and on, and always to be just as exciting as at the very first, and it wouldn't! We had got to the point where we couldn't be interested in anything any more. We were as little ones unable to prop their eyelids open and yet quarreling with bed. We were surfeited, but not satisfied. We sat there and pouted because there wasn't any more, and yet we couldn't but yawn at the act before us. We were mad at ourselves, and mad at everybody else. We clambered down the rattling bedslats seats, sour and sullen. We didn't want to look at the animals; we didn't want to do this, and we didn't want to do that. We whined and snarled, and wriggled and shook ourselves with temper, and we got a good hard slap, side of the head, right before everybody, and then we yelled as if we were being killed alive.

"Now, mister, if I ever take you any place again, you'll know it. I'd be ashamed of myself if I was you. Hush up! Hush up, I tell you. Now you mark. You're never going to the show again. Do you hear me? Never! I mean it. You're never going again."

But at eventide there was light. After supper, after a little rest and a good deal of food, while chopping the kindling for morning (it's wonderful how useful employ tends to induce a cheerful view of life) out of her dazzling treasure-heap of jewels, Memory took up, one after another, a glowing recollection and viewed it with delight. The evening performance, the one all lighted up with bunches and bunches of lights, was a-preparing, and in the gentle breeze the far-off music waved as it had been a flag. A harsh and rumbling noise as of heavy timbers falling tore through the tissue of sweet sounds. The horses in the barn next door screamed in their stalls to hear it. Ages and ages ago, on distant wind-swept plains their ancestors had hearkened to that hunting-cry, and summoned up their valor and their speed. It still thrilled in the blood of these patient slaves of man, though countless generations of them had never even so much as seen a lion.

"And is that all the difference, pa, that the lion roars at night and the ostrich in the daytime?"

Out on the back porch in the deepening dusk we sat, with eyes relaxed and dreaming, and watched the stars that powdered the dark sky. Before our inward vision passed in review the day of splendor and renown. We sighed, at last, but it was the happy sigh of him who has full dined. Ambition was digesting. In our turn, when we grew up, we, too, were to do the deeds of high emprise. We were to be somebody.

(I never heard of anybody sitting up to see the show depart. And yet it seems to me that would be the best time to run off with it.)

The next day we visited the lots. It was no dream. See the litter that mussed up the place.

We were all there. None had heard the man that runs the show say genially: "Yes, I think we can arrange to take you with us." Here was the ring; here the tent-pole holes, and here a scrap of paper torn from a hoop the bareback rider leaped through . . . . Oh, now I know what I was going to tell you that the clown said. The comicalest thing!

He picked up one of these hoops and began to sniffle.

So the ring-master asked him what he was crying about.

"I - I -was thinking of my mother. Smf! My good old mother!"

So the ring-master asked him what made him think of his mother.

"This." And he held up the paper-covered hoop.

The ring-master couldn't see how that put the clown in

mind of his mother. He was awful dumb, that man.

"It looks just like the pancakes she used to make for us."

Well, sir, we just hollered and laughed at that. And after we had quieted down a little, the ringmaster says: "As big as that?"

"Bigger," says the clown. "Why, she used to make 'em so big we used 'em for bedclothes."

"Indeed" (Just like that. He took it all in, just as if it was so.)

"Oh, my, yes! I mind one time I was sleeping with my little brother, and I waked up just as cold - Brr! But I was cold!"

"But how could that be, sir? You just now said you had pancakes for bedclothes."

"Yes, but my little brother got hungry in the night, and et up all the cover."

Laugh? Why, they screamed. Me? I thought I'd just about go up. But the ring master never cracked a smile. He didn't see the joke at all.

Good-by, old clown, friend of our childhood, goodby, good-by forever! And you, our other friend, the street parade, must you go, too? And you, the gorgeous show-bills, must you tread the path toward the sundown? Good-by! Good-by! In that dreary land where you are going, the Kingdom of the Ausgespielt, it may comfort you to recollect the young hearts you

have made happy in the days that were, but never more
can be again.

THE COUNTY FAIR

Whether or not the name had an influence on the weather, I don't know. Perhaps it did rain some years, but, as I remember, County Fair time seems to have had a sky perfectly cloudless, with its blue only a little dulled around the edges where it came close to the ground and the dust settled on it. Things far off were sort of hazy, but that might have been the result of the bonfires of leaves we had been having evenings after supper. In Fair weather, when the sun had been up long enough to get a really good start, it was right warm, but in the shade it was cool, and nights and mornings there was a chill in the air that threatened worse things to come.

The harvest is past, the summer is ended. Down cellar the swing-shelf is cram-jam full of jellyglasses, and jars of fruit. Out on the hen-house roof are drying what, when the soap-box wagon was first built, promised barrels and barrels of nuts to be brought up with the pitcher of cider for our comforting in the long winter evenings, but what turns out, when the shucks are off, to be a poor, pitiful half-peck, daily depleted by the urgent necessity of finding out if they are dry enough yet. Folks are picking apples, and Koontz's cider-mill is in full operation. (Do you know any place where a fellow can get some nice long straws?) Out in the fields are champagne-colored pyramids, each with a pale-gold heap of corn beside it, and the good black earth is dotted with orange blobs that promise pumpkin-pies for Thanksgiving Day. No. Let me look again. Those aren't pie-pumpkins; those are cow-pumpkins, and if you want to see something kind of pitiful, I'll show you Abe Bethard chopping up one of those yellow globes -with what, do you suppose? With the cavalry saber his daddy used at Gettysburg.

The harvest is past, the summer is ended. As a result of all the good feeding and the outdoor air we have had for three or four months past, the strawberry shortcakes, and cherry-pies, and green peas, and new potatoes, and string beans, and roasting-ears, and all such garden-stuff, and the fresh eggs, broken into the skillet before Speckle gets done cackling, and the cockerels we pick off the roost Saturday evenings (you see, we're thinning 'em out; no sense in keeping all of 'em over winter) - as a result, I say, of all this good eating, and the outdoor life, and the necessity of stirring around a little lively these days we feel pretty good. And yet we get kind of low in our minds, too. The harvest is past, the summer is ended. It's gone, the good playtime when we didn't have to go to school, when the only foot-covering we wore was a rag around one big toe or the other; the days when we could stay in swimming all day long except mealtimes; the days of Sabbath-school picnics and excursions to the Soldiers' Home - it's gone. The harvest is past, the summer is ended. The green and leafy things have heard the word, and most of them are taking it pretty seriously, judging by their looks. But the maples and some more of them, particularly the maples, with daredevil recklessness, have resolved, as it were, to die with their boots on, and flame out in such violent and unbelievable colors that we feel obliged to take testimony in certain outrageous cases, and file away the exhibits in the Family Bible where nobody will bother them. The harvest is past, the summer is ended. Rainy days you can see how played-out and forlorn the whole world looks. But at Fair time, when the sun shines bright, it appears right cheerful.

It seems to me the Fair lasted three days. One of them was a holiday from school, I know, and unless I'm wrong, it wasn't on the first day, because then they were getting the things in, and it wasn't on the last day, because then they were taking the things out, so it must have been on the middle day, when everybody went. Charley Wells had both the depot 'buses out with "County FAIR" painted on muslin hung on the sides. The Cornet Band rode all round town in one, and so on over to the "scene of the festivities" as the Weekly Examiner very aptly put it, and then both 'buses stood out in front of the American House, waiting for passengers, with Dinny Enright calling out: "This sway t' the Fair Groun's! Going RIGHT over!" Only he always waited till he got a good load before he turned a wheel. (Dinny's foreman at the chair factory now. Did you know that? Doing fine. Gets $15 a week, and hasn't drunk a drop for nearly two years.)

Everybody goes the middle day of the Fair, everybody that you ever did know or hear tell of. You'll be going along, kind of half-listening to the man selling Temperance Bitters, and denouncing the other bitters because they have "al-cue-hawl" in them, and "al-cue-hawl will make you drunk," (which is perfectly true), and kind of half-listening to the man with the electric machine, declaring: "Ground is the first conductor; water is the second conductor," and you'll be thinking how slippery the grass is to walk on, when a face in the crowd will, as it were, sting your memory. "I ought to know that man," says you to yourself. "Now, who the mischief is he? Barker? No, 't isn't Barker, Barkdull? No. Funny I can't think of his name. Begins with B I'm pretty certain." And you trail along after him, as if you were a detective, sort of keeping out of his sight, and yet every once in a while getting a good look at him. "Mmmmmm!" says you. "What is that fellow's name? Why, sure. McConica." And you walk up to him and stick out your hand while he's gassing with somebody, and there's that smile on your face that says: "I know you but you don't know me," and he takes it in a limp sort of fashion, and starts to say: "You have the advantage of - " when, all of a sudden, he grabs your hand as if he were going to jerk your arm out of its socket and beat you over the head with the bloody end, and shouts out: "Why, HELLO, Billy! Well, suffering Cyrus and all hands round! Hold still a second and let me look at you. Gosh darn your hide, where you been for so long? I though you'd clean evaporated off the face the earth. Why, how AIR you? How's everything? That's good. Let me make you acquainted with my wife. Molly, this is Mr. - " But she says: "Now don't you tell me what his name is. Let me think. Why, Willie Smith! Well, of all things! Why, how you've changed! Honest, I wouldn't have knowed you. Do you mind the time we went sleigh-ridin' the whole posse of us, and got upset down there by Hanks's place?" And then you start in on "D' you mind?" and "Don't you recollect?" and you talk about the old school-days, and who's married, and who's moved out to Kansas, and who's got the Elias Hoover place now, and how Ella Trimble - You know Ella Diefenbaugh, old Jake Diefenbaugh's daughter, the one that lisped. Course you do. Well, she married Ed Trimble, and he died along in the early part of the summer. Typhoid. Was

Eugene Wood

getting well but he took a relapse, and went off like that! And now she's left with three little ones, and they guess poor Ella has a pretty hard time making out. And this old schoolmate that you start to tell a funny story about is dead, and the freckle-faced boy with the buck teeth that put the rabbit in the teacher's desk, he's dead, too, and the boy that used to cry in school when they read:

> "Give me three grains of corn, mother,
> Only three grains o f corn;
> To save what little life I have, mother,
> Till the coming o f the morn."

well, he studied law with old judge Rodehaver, and got to be Prosecuting Attorney, but he took to drinking - politics, you know - and now he's just gone to the dogs. Smart as a steel-trap, and bright as a dollar. Oh, a terrible pity! A terrible pity. And as you hear the fate of one after another of the happy companions of your childhood, and the sadness of life comes over you, they start to tell something that makes you laugh again. I tell you. Did you ever see one of these concave glasses, such as the artists use when they want to get an idea of how a picture looks all together as a whole, and not as an assemblage of parts? Well, what the concave glass is to a picture, so such talk is to life. It sort of draws it all together, and you see it as a whole, its sunshine and its shadow, its laughter and its tears, its work and its play, its past and its present. But not its future. The Good Man has mercifully hidden that from us.

It does a body good to get such a talk once in a while.

And there are the young fellows and the girls. This

young gentleman in the rimless eye-glasses, who is now beginning to "go out among 'em" the last time you saw him was in meeting when Elder Drown was preaching, and my gentleman stood up in the seat and shouted shrilly: "'T ain't at all, man. 'T ain't at all!" And this sweet girl-graduate - the last time you saw her was just after Becky Daly, in the vain effort to "peacify" the squalling young one, had given her a fresh egg to play with. I kind o' like the looks of the younger generation of girls. But I don't know about the young fellows. They look to me like a trifling lot. Nothing like what they were in our young days. I don't see but what us old codgers had better hold on a while longer to the County Clerk's office, and the Sheriff's office, and the Probate judgeship, and the presidency of the National Bank. It wouldn't be safe to trust the destinies of the country in the hands of such heedless young whiffets. Engaged to be married! Oh, get out! What? Those babies?

I kept awake most of the time the man was lecturing on: "The Republic: Will it Endure?" but I don't remember that he said anything in it about the crops. (We can't go 'round meeting the folks all day. We really must give a glance at the exhibition.) And I am one of those who hold to the belief that while the farmers can raise ears of corn as long as from your elbow to your fingertips, as big 'round as a rollingpin, and set with grains as regular and even as an eight-dollar set of artificial teeth; as long as they grow potatoes the size of your foot, and such pretty oats and wheat, and turnips, and squashes, and onions, and apples and all kinds of truck, and raise them not only in increasing size but increasing quantities to the acre I feel as if the Republic would last the year out anyway. Not that I have any notion that mere material prosperity will make and keep us a free people, but it goes to show that the farmers are not plodding along, doing as their fathers did before them, but that they are reading and studying, and taking advantage of modern methods. There are two ways of increasing your income. One is by enlarging your output, and the other is by enlarging your share of the proceeds from the sale of that output. The Grand Dukes will not always run this country. The farmers saved the Union once by dying for it; they will save it again by living for it.

The scientific fellows tell us that we have not nearly reached the maximum of yield to the acre of crops that are harvested once a year, but in regard to the crops that are harvested twice a day it looks to me as if we were doing fairly well. Nowadays we hardly know what is meant by the expression, "Spring poor." It is a sinister phrase, and tells a story of the old, cruel days when farmers begrudged their cattle the little bite they ate in wintertime, so that when the grass came again the poor creatures would fall over trying to crop it. They were so starved and weak that, as the saying went, they had to lean up against the fence to breathe. They don't do that way now, as one look at the fine, sleek cows will show you. A cow these days is a different sort of a being, her coat like satin, and her udder generous, compared with the wild-eyed things with burrs in their tails, and their flanks crusted with filth, their udders the size of a kid glove, and yielding such a little dab of milk and for such a short period. Hear the dairymen boast now of the miraculous yearly yield in pounds of butter and milk, and when they say: "You've got to treat a cow as if she were a lady," it sounds like good sense.

Pigs are naturally so untidy about their persons, and

have such shocking table-manners that it seems difficult to treat a sow like a lady, but that one in the pen yonder, with her litter of sucking pigs, seems very interesting. Come, let's have a look. Aren't the little pigs dear things? I'd like to climb in and take one of them up to pet it; do you s'pose she'd mind it if I did? I can see decided improvement in the modern hogs over old Mose Batcheller's. If you remember, his were what were known as "razorbacks." They could go like the wind, and the fence was not made that could stop them. If they couldn't root under it, they could turn themselves sidewise and slide through between the rails. It was told me that, failing all else, they could give their tails a swing - you remember the big balls of mud they used to have on their tails' ends - they could swing their tails after the manner of an athlete throwing the hammer, and fly over the top of the tallest stake-and-rider fence ever put up. I don't know whether this is the strict truth or not, but it is what was told me as a little boy, and I don't think people would wilfully deceive an innocent child.

The pigs nowaday aren't as smart as that, but they cut up better at hog-killing time. They aren't quite so trim; indeed, they are nothing but cylinders of meat, whittled to a point at the front end, and set on four pegs, but as you lean on the top-rail of the pens out at the County Fair and look down upon them, you can picture in your mind, without much effort, ham, and sidemeat, and bacon, and spare-ribs, and smoked shoulder, and head-cheese, and liver-wurst, and sausages, and glistening white lard for crullers and pie-crust - Yes, I think pigs are right interesting. I know they've got Scripture for it, the folks that think it is wrong to eat pork, but somehow I feel sorry for them; they miss such a lot, not only in the eating line, but other ways. They are

Eugene Wood

always being persecuted, and harassed, and picked at. Whereas the pork-fed man, it seems to me, sort of hankers to be picked at. It gives him a good chance to slap somebody slonchways. He feels better after he has seen his persecutors go away with a cut lip, and fingering of their teeth to see if they're all there.

You'll just have to take me gently but firmly by the sleeve and lead me past the next exhibit, the noisy one, where there's so much cackling and crowing. I give you fair warning that if you get me started talking about chickens, the County Fair will have to wait till some other time. I don't know much about ducks, and geese, and guinea-hens, and pea-fowl, and turkeys, but chickens -Why, say. We had a hen once (Plymouth Rock she was; we called her Henrietta), and honestly, that hen knew more than some folks. One time she - all right. I'll hush. Let's go in here.

I don't remember whether the pies, and cakes, and canned fruit, and such are in Pomona Hall or the Fine Arts Hall. Fine Arts Hall I think. They ought to be. I speak to be one of the judges that give out the premiums in this department. I'd be generous and let somebody else do the judging of the cakes, because I don't care much for cake. Oh, I can manage to choke it down, but I haven't the expert knowledge, practical and scientific, that I have in the matter of pie. I'd bear my share of the work when it came to the other things, jellies and preserves, and pies, but not cake. Wouldn't know just exactly how to go at it in the matter of jellies. I'd take a glass of currant, and hold it up to the light to note its crimson glory. And I'd lift off the waxed paper top and peer in, and maybe give the jelly a shake. And then I'd take a spoon and taste, closing my eyes so as to appear to deliberate - they'd roll up in an ecstacy anyhow - and I'd smack my lips, and say: "Mmmmm!" very thoughtfully, and set the glass back, and write down in my book my judgment, which would invariably be: "First Prize." Because if there is anything on top of this green earth that I think is just about right, it is currant jelly. Grape jelly is nice, and crab-apple jelly has its good points, and quince jelly is very delicate, but there is something about currant jelly that seems to touch the spot. Quince preserves are good if there is enough apple with the quince, and watermelon preserves are a great favorite, not because they are so much better tasting, but because the lucent golden cubes in the spicy syrup appeal so to the eye. But if you want to know what I think is really good eating in the preserve line, you just watch my motions when I come to the tomato preserves, these little fig-tomatoes, and see how quick the red card is put on them. Yes, indeed. It's been a long time, hasn't it? since you had any tomato-preserves, you that haven't been "Back Home" lately.

It's no great trick to put up other fruit so that it will keep, but I'd look the canned tomatoes over pretty carefully, and if I saw that one lady had not only put them up so that they hadn't turned foamy, but had also succeeded with green corn, and that other poser, string beans, I'd give her first premium, because I'd know she was a first-rate housekeeper, and a careful woman, and one that deserved encouragement.

But I'd save myself for the pies. I can tell a rich, short, flaky crust, and I can tell the kind that is as brown as a dried apple, and tough as the same on the top, and sad and livery on the bottom. And I know about fillings, how thick they ought to be, and how they ought to be seasoned, and all. Particularly pumpkin-pies, because I had early advantages that way that very few other boys had. I was allowed to scrape the crock that had held the pumpkin for the pies. So that's how I know as much as I do.

I suppose, however, when all is said and done, that there is no pie that can quite come up to an apple-pie. You take nice, short crust that's been worked up with ice-water, and line the tin with it, and fill it heaping with sliced, tart apples -not sauce. Mercy, no! - and sweeten them just right, and put on a lump of butter, and some allspice, and perhaps a clove, and a little lemon peel, and then put on the cover, and trim off the edge, and pinch it up in scallops, and draw a couple of leaves in the top with a sharp knife, and have the oven just right, and set it in there, and I tell you that when ma opens the oven-door to see how the pie is coming on, there distils through the house such a perfume that you cry out in a choking voice: "Say! Ain't dinner 'most ready?"

But I fully recognize the fact that very often our judgment is warped by feeling, and I am inclined to believe that even the undoubted merit of the apple-pie would not prevail against a vinegar-pie, if such should be presented to me for my decision. A vinegar-pie? Well, it has a top and bottom crust, the same as any other pie, but its filling is made of vinegar, diluted with water to the proper degree of sub-acidity, sweetened with molasses, thickened with flour, and all baked as any other pie. You smile at its crude simplicity, and wonder why I should favor it. To you it doesn't tell the story that it does to me. It doesn't take you back in imagination to "the airly days," when folks came over the mountains in covered wagons, and settled in the Western Reserve, leaving behind them all the civilization of their day, and its comforts, parting from relatives and friends, knowing full well that in this life they never more should look upon their faces - leaving everything behind to make a new home in the western wilds.

Is was a land of promise that they came to. The virgin soil bore riotously. There were fruit-trees in the forest that Johnny Appleseed had planted on his journeyings. The young husband could stand in his dooryard and kill wild turkeys with his rifle. They fed to loathing on venison, and squirrels, and all manner of game, and once in a great while they had the luxury of salt pork. They were well-nourished, but sometimes they pined for that which was more than mere food. They hungered for that which should be to the meals' victuals what the flower is to the plant.

"I whoosh't - I woosh't was so we could hev pie," sighed one such. (Let us call him Uriah Kinney. I think that sounds as if it were his name.

"Land's sakes!" snapped his wife, exasperated that he should be thinking of the same thing that she was. "Land's sakes! Haow d' ye s'pose I kin make a pie when I hain't got e'er a thing to make it aout o'? You gimme suthirnn to make it aout o', an' you see haow quick - "

"I ain't a-faultinn ye, Mary Ann," interposed Uriah gently. "I know haow 't is. I was on'y tellin' ye. I git I git a kind o' hum'sick sometimes. 'Pears like as if I sh'd feel more resigned like . . . . Don't ye cry, Mary Ann. I know, I know. You feel julluk I do 'baout back home, an' all luk that."

O woman! When the heft of thy intellect is thrown against a problem, something has got to give. Not long after, Uriah sits down to dinner, and can hardly ask a blessing, he has to swallow so. A pie is on the table!

"Gosh, Mary Ann, but this is good!" says he, holding out his hand for the third piece. "This is lickinn good!" And he celebrates her achievement far and wide.

"My Mary Ann med me a pie t' other day, was the all-firedest best pie I ever et."

"Med you what?"

"Med me a pie."

"Pie? Whutch talkinn' baout? Can't git nummore pies naow. Frot 's all gin aout."

"I golly, she med it just the same. Smartest woman y' ever see." The man dribbled at the mouth.

"What sh' make it aout o'?"

"Vinegar an' worter, I think she said. I d' know 's I ever et anythinn I relished julluk that. My Mary Ann, tell yew! She's 'baout's smart 's they make 'em."

I wish I knew who she really was whom I have called Mary Ann Kinney, she that made the first vinegar-pie. I wish I knew where her grave is that I might lay upon it a bunch of flowers, such as she knew and liked - sweet-william, and phlox, and larkspur, and wild columbine. It couldn't make it up to her for all the hardships she underwent when she was bringing up a family in that wild, western country, and especially that fall when they all had the "fever 'n' ager" so bad, Uriah and the twins chilling one day, and Hiram and Sophronia Jane the next, and she just as miserable as any of them, but keeping up somehow, God only knows how. It couldn't make it up to her, but as I laid the pretty posies against the leaning headstone on which is written:

"A Loving Wife , a Mother Dear,
Faithful Friend Lies Buried Here."

I believe she 'd get word of it somehow, and understand what I was trying to say by it.

I'll ask to be let off the committee that judges the rest of the exhibits in the Fine Arts Hall, the quilts and the Battenberg, and the crocheting, and such. I know the Log Cabin pattern, and the Mexican Feather pattern, and I think I could make out to tell the Hen-and-Chickens pattern of quilts, but that's as much as ever. And as to the real, hand-painted views of fruit-cake, and grapes and apples on a red table-cloth, I am one of those that can't make allowances for the fact that she only took two terms. I call to mind one picture that Miss Alvalou Ashbaker made of her pap, old "Coonrod" Ashbaker. The Lord knows he was a "humbly critter," but he wasn't as "humbly" as she made him out to be, with his eyes bulging out of his head as if he was choking on a fishbone. And, instead of her dressing him up in his Sunday clothes, I wish I may never see the back of my neck if that girl didn't paint him in a red-and-black barred flannel shirt, with porcelain buttons on it! And his hair looked as if the calf had been at it. Wouldn't you think somebody would have told her? And that isn't all. She got the premium!

Neither am I prepared to pass judgment on the fancy penmanship displayed by Professor Swope, framed elegantly in black walnut, and gilt, depicting a bounding deer, all made out of hair-line, shaded spirals, done with his facile pen. (No wonder a deer can jump so, with all those springs inside him.) Professor Swope writes visiting cards for you, wonderful birds done in flourishes and holding ribbons in their bills. He puts your name on the ribbon place. Neatest and tastiest thing you can imagine. I like to watch him do it, but it makes me feel unhappy, somehow. I never was much of a scribe, and it's too late for me to learn now.

I don't feel so downcast when I examine the specimens of writing done by the children of District No. 34. I can just see the young ones working at home on these things, with their tongues stuck out of one corner of their mouths.

"Rome was not built in a day
Rome was not built in a day
Rome was not built in a day"

and so on, bearing down hard on the downstroke of the curve in the capital "R," and clubbing the end of the little "t." And in the higher grades, they toil over "An Original Social Letter," describing to an imaginary correspondent a visit to Crystal Lake, or the Magnetic Springs. I can hear them mourn: "What shall I say next?" and "Ma, make Effie play some place else, won't you? She jist joggles the table like everything. Now, see what you done! Now I got to write it all over again. No, I cain't 'scratch it out. How'd it look to the County Fair all scratched out? Plague take it all!"

The same hands have done maps of North and South America, and red-and-blue ink pictures of the circulation of the blood. It does beat all how smart the young ones are nowadays. I could no more draw off a picture of the circulation of the blood - get it right, I mean - why, I wouldn't attempt it.

I am kind of mixed up in my recollection of the hall right next to the Fine Arts. You know it had two doors in each end. Sometimes I can see the central space between the doors, roped off and devoted to sewing-machines with persons demonstrating that they ran as light as a feather, and how it was no trouble at all to tuck and gather, and fell; to organs, which struck me with amaze, because by some witchcraft (octave coupler, I think they called it) the man could play on keys that he didn't touch, and pianos, whereon young ladies were prevailed to perform "Silvery Waves" - that's a lovely piece, I think, don't you? - and

"Listen to the mocking-bird, TEE-die-eedle-DONG
Lisen to the mocking-bird, teedle-eedle-EE-dle
DONG
The mocking-bird still singing oer her grave,
toomatooral-oo-cal-LEE!"

And then again I can see that central, roped-off space given over to reckless deviltry, sheer impudent, brazen-faced, bold, discipline-defying er - er - wicked-ness. I had heard that people did things like that, but this was the first time I had ever caught a glimpse of such carryings-on in the broad open daylight, right before everybody. I stood there and watched them for hours, expecting every minute to see fire fall from heaven on them and burn up every son and daughter of Belial. But it didn't.

Eugene Wood

I seem to recollect that it was a hot day, and that, tucked away where not a breath of air could get to them, were three fellows in their shirtsleeves, one playing on an organ, one on a yellow clarinet, and one on a fiddle. Every chance he could get, the fiddler would say to the organist: "Gimme A, please," and saw away trying to get into some sort of tune, but the catgut was never twisted that would hold to pitch with the perspiration dribbling down his fingers in little rills. The clarinet man looked as if he wanted to cry, and he had to twitter his eyelids all the time to keep the sweat from blinding him, and every once in a while, his soggy reed would let go of a squawk that sounded like a scared chicken. But the organ groaned on unrelentingly, and the tune didn't matter so much as the rhythm which was kept up as regular as a clock, whack! whack! whack! whack! And there were two or three other fellows with badges on that went around shouting: "Select your podners for the next quadrille! One more couple wanted right over here!"

Dancing. M-hm.

The fiddler "called off" and chanted to the tune, with his mouth on one side: "Sullootch podners! First couple forward and back. Side couples the same. Doe see do-o-o-o. Al-lee-man LEFT! Ballunce ALL! Saweeny the corners!" I don't know whether I get the proper order of these commands or not, or whether my memory serves me as to their effect, but it seems to me that at "Bal-lunce ALL!" the ladies demurely teetered, first on one foot and then on the other, like a frozen-toed rooster, while the gents fairly tore themselves apart with grape-vine twists and fancy steps, and slapped the dust out of the cracks in the floor. When it came to "SaWEENG your podners!" the room billowed with flying skirts, and the ladies squealed like anything. It made you a little dizzy to watch them do "Graaan' right and left," and you could understand how those folks felt - there were always one or two in each set - who had to be hauled this way and that, not sure whether they were having a good time or not, but hoping they were, their faces set in a sickly grin, while their foreheads wrinkled into a puzzled: "How's that? I didn't quite catch that last remark" expression. I don't know if it affected you in the same way that it did me, but after I had stood there for a time and watched those young men and women thus wasting the precious moments that dropped like priceless pearls into the ocean of Eternity, and were lost irrevocably, young, men and women giving themselves up to present enjoyment without one serious thought in their minds as to who was going to wash the supper dishes, or what would happen if the house took fire while they were away I say I do not know how the sight of such reckless frivolity affected you, but I know that after so long a time my face would get all cramped up from wearing a grin, and I'd have to go out and look at the reapers and binders to rest myself so I could come back and look some. There are two things that you simply have to do at the County Fair, or you aren't right sure you've been. One is to drink a glass of sweet cider just from the press, (which, I may say in passing, is an over-rated luxury. Cider has to be just the least bit "frisky" to be good. I don't mean hard, but" frisky." You know). And the other is to buy a whip, if it is only the, little toy, fifteen-cent kind. On the next soap-box to the old fellow that comes every year to sell pictorial Bibles and red, plush-covered albums, the old fellow in the green slippers that talks as if he were just ready to drop off to sleep - on the next soap-box to him is the man that sells the whips. You can buy one for a dollar, two for a dollar, or four for a dollar, but not one for fifty cents, or one for a quarter. Don't ask me why, for I don't know. I am just stating the facts. It can't be done, for I've seen it tried, and if you keep up the attempt too long, the whip-man will lose all patience with your unreasonableness, and tell you to go 'long about your business if you've got any, and not bother the life and soul out of him, because he won't sell anything but a dollar's worth of whips, and that's all there is about it.

He sells other things, handsaws, and pencils, and mouth-harps, and two knives for a quarter, of such pure steel that he whittles shavings off a wire nail with 'em, and is particular to hand you the very identical knife he did it with. He has jewelry, though I don't suppose you could cut a wire nail with it. You might, at that.

To him approaches a boy.

"Got 'ny collar-buttons?"

"Well, now, I'll just look and see. Here's a beautiful rolled-plate gold watch-chain, with an elegant jewel charm. Lovely blue jewel." He dangles the chain and its rich glass pendant, and it certainly does look fine. "That'd cost you $2.50 at the store. How'd that strike you ?"

"Hpm. I want a collar-button."

"Well, now, you hold on a minute. Lemme look again. Ah, here's a package 'at orta have some in it. Yes, sir, here's four of 'em, enough to last you a lifetime; front, back, and both sleeves, the kind that flips and don't tear the buttonholes. Well, by ginger! Now, how'd that git in here, I want to know? That gold ring? Well, I don't care. It'll have to go with the collar-buttons. Tell you what I'll do with you: I'll let you have this elegant solid gold rolled-plate watch-chain and jewel, this elegant, solid gold ring to git married with - Hay? How about it? - and these four collar-buttons for - for - twenty-five cents, or a quarter of a dollar."

That boy never took that quarter out of his breeches pocket. It just jumped out of itself. But I see that you are getting the fidgets. You're hoping that I'll come to the horse-racing pretty soon. You want to have it all brought back to you, the big, big race-track which, as you remember it now, must have been about the next size smaller than the earth's orbit around the sun. You want me to tell about the old farmer with the bunch of timothy whiskers under his chin that gets his old jingling wagon on the track just before a heat is to be trotted, and all the people yell at him: "Take him out!" You want me to tell how the trotters looked walking around in their dusters, with the eye-holes bound with red braid, and how the drivers of the sulkies sat with the tails of their horses tucked under one leg. Well, I'm not going to do anything of the kind, and if you don't like it, you can go to the box-office and demand your money back. I hope you'll get it. First place, I don't know anything about racing, and consequently I don't believe it's a good thing for the country. All I know is, that some horses can go faster than others, but which are the fastest ones I can't tell by the looks, though I have tried several times . . . . I did not walk back. I bought a round-trip ticket. They will tell you that these events at the County Fair tend to improve the breed of horses. So they do - of fast horses. But the fast horses are no good. They can't any of them go as fast as a nickel trolley-car when it gets out where there aren't any houses. And they not only are no good; they're a positive harm. You know and I know that just as soon as a man gets cracked after fast horses, it's good-by John with him.

In the next place, I wouldn't mind it if it was only interesting to me. But it isn't. It bores me to death. You sit there and sit there trying to keep awake while the drivers jockey and jockey, scheming to get the advantage of the other fellow, and the bell rings so many times for them to come back after you think: "They're off this time, sure," that you get sick of hearing it. And when they do get away, why, who can tell which horse is in the lead? On the far side of the track they don't appear to do anything but poke along, and once in a while some fool horse will "break" and that's annoying. And then when they come into the stretch, the other folks that see you with the field-glasses, keep nudging you and asking: "Who 's ahead, mister? Hay? Who's ahead?" And it's ruinous to the voice to yell: "Go it! Go it! Go IT, ye devil, you!" with your throat all clenched that way and your face as red as a turkey-gobbler's. And that second when they are going under the wire, and the horse you rather like is about a nose behind the other one that you despise - Oh, tedious, very tedious. Ho hum, Harry! If I wasn't engaged, I wouldn't marry. Did you think to put a saucer of milk out for the kitty before you locked up the house?

No. Horse-racing bores me to death, and as I am one of the charter members of the Anti-Other-Folks-Enjoyment Society, organized to stop people from amusing themselves in ways that we don't care for, you can readily see that it is a matter of principle with me to ignore horseracing, and not to give it so much encouragement as would come from mentioning it.

If you're so interested in improving the breed of horses by competitive contests, what 's the matter with that one where the prize is $5 for the team that can haul the heaviest load on a stoneboat, straight pulling? Pile on enough stones to build a house, pretty near, and the owner of the team, a young fellow with a face like Keats, goes "Ck! Ck! Ck! Geet . . . ep . . . thah BILL! Geet ep, Doll-ay!" and cracks his whip, and kisses with his mouth, and the horses dance and tug, and jump around and strain till the stone-boat slides on the grass, and then men climb on until the load gets so heavy that the team can't budge it. Then another team tries, and so on, the competitors jawing and jowering at each other with: "Ah, that ain't fair! That ain't fair! They started it sideways."

"That don't make no difference."

"Yes, it does, too, make a difference. Straight ahead four inches. that's the rule."

"Well, didn't they go straight ahead four inches? What's a matter with ye?"

"I'll darn soon show ye what's the matter with me, you come any o' your shenanigan around here."

" Mighty ready to accuse other folks o' shenannigan, ain't ye? For half a cent I'd paste you in the moot."

"Now, boys! Now boys! None o' that."

Lots more excitement than a horse-race. Lots more

improving to the mind, and beneficial to the country.

And if you hanker after the human element of skill, what's the matter with the contest where the women see who can hitch up a horse the quickest? Didn't you have your favorite picked out from the start? I did. She was about thirteen years old, dressed in an organdie, and I think she had light blue ribbons flying from her hat, light blue or pink, I forget which. Her pa helped her unharness, and you could tell by the way he look-at her that he thought she was about the smartest young one for her age in her neighborhood. (You ought to hear her play "General Grant's Grand March" on the organ he bought for her, a fine organ with twenty-four stops and two full sets of reeds, and a mirror in the top, and places to set bouquets and all.) There was a woman in the contest that seemed, by her actions, to think that the others were just wasting their time competing with her, but when they got the word "Go!" (Old Nate Wells was the judge; he sold out the livery-stable business to Charley, you recollect) her horse backed in wrong, and she got the harness all twisty-ways, and everything went bewitched. And wasn't she provoked, though? Served her right, I say. A little woman beside her was the first to jump into her buggy, and drive off with a strong inhalation of breath, and that nipping together of the lips that says: "A-a-ah! I tell ye!" The little girl that we picked out was hopping around like a scared cockroach, and her pa seemed to be saying: "Now, keep cool! Keep cool! Don't get flustered," but when another woman drove off, I know she almost cried, she felt so bad. But she was third, and when she and her pa drove around the ring, the people clapped her lots more than the other two. I guess they must have picked her for a favorite the same as you and I did. Bless her heart! I hope she got a good man when she grew up.

Around back of the Old Settlers' Cabin, where they have the relics, the spinning-wheel, the flax-hackle, and the bunch of dusty tow that nobody knows how to spin in these degenerate days; the old flint-lock rifle, and the powder-horn; the tinder-box, and the blue plate, "more'n a hundred years old;" the dog-irons, tongs, poker, and turkey-wing of an ancient fireplace - around back of the Old Settlers' Cabin all the early part of the day a bunch of dirty canvas has been dangling from a rope stretched between two trees. It was fenced off from the curious, but after dinner a stranger in fringy trousers and a black singlet went around picking out big, strong, adventurous young fellows to stand about the wooden ring fastened to the bottom of the bunch of canvas, which went over the smoke-pipe of a sort of underground furnace in which a roaring fire had been built. As the hot air filled the great bag, it was the task of these helpers to shake out the wrinkles and to hold it down. Older and wiser ones forbade their young ones to go near it. Supposing it should explode; what then? But we have always wanted to fly away up into the air, and what did we come to the Fair for, if not for excitement? The balloon swells out amazingly fast, and when the guy-ropes are loosened and drop to the ground, the elephantine bag clumsily lunges this way and that, causing shrill squeals from those who fear to be whelmed in it. The man in the singlet tosses kerosene into the furnace from a tin cup, and you can see the tall flames leap upward from the flue into the balloon. It grows tight as a drum.

"Watch your horses!" he calls out. There is a pause . . . "Let go all!" The mighty shape shoots up twenty feet or so, and the man in the singlet darts to the corner to cut a lone detaining rope. As he runs he sheds his fringy trousers.

"Good-by, everybody!" he cries out, and the sinister possibilities in that phrase are overlooked in the wonder at seeing him lurch upward through the air, all glorious in black tights and yellow breech-clout. Up and up he soars above the tree-tops, and the wind gently wafts him along, a pendant to a dusky globe hanging in the sky. He is just a speck now swaying to and fro. The globe plunges upward; the pendant drops like a shot. There is a rustling sound. It is the intake of the breath of horror from ten thousand pairs of lungs. Look! Look! The edges of the parachute ruffle, and then it blossoms out like an opening flower. It bounces on the air a little, and rocking gently sinks like thistle-down behind the woods.

It is all over. The Fair is over. Let's go home. Isn't it wonderful though, what men can do? You'll see; they'll be flying like birds, one of these days. That's what we little boys think, but we overhear old Nate Wells say to Tom Slaymaker, as we pass them: "Well, I d' know. I d' know 's these here b'loon ascensions is worth the money they cost the 'Sociation. I seen so many of 'em, they don't interest me nummore. 'Less, o' course, sumpun should happen to the feller."

CHRISTMAS BACK HOME

It was the time of year when the store windows are mighty interesting. Plotner's bakery, that away, 'way back in the summer-time, was an ice-cream saloon, showed a plaster man in the window, with long, white whiskers, in top boots and a brown coat and peaked hat, all trimmed with fur, and carrying a little pinetree with arsenical foliage. Over his head dangled a thicket of canes hanging by their crooks from a twine string stretched across. They were made of candy striped spirally in red and white. There were candy men and women in the window, and chocolate mice with red eyes, and a big cake, all over frosting, with a candy preacher on it marrying a candy man and lady. The little children stood outside, with their joggerfies, and arithmetics, and spellers, and slates bound in red flannel under their arms, and swallowed hard as they looked. Whenever anybody went in for a penny's worth of yeast and opened the door, that had a bell fastened to it so that Mrs. Plotner could hear in the back room, and come to wait on the customer, the smell of wintergreen and peppermint and lemonsticks and hot taffy gushed out so strong that they couldn't swallow fast enough, but stood there choking and dribbling at the mouth.

Brown's shoe store exhibited green velvet slippers with deers' heads on them, and Galbraith's windows were

Eugene Wood

hung with fancy dressgoods, and handkerchiefs with dogs' heads in the corners; but, next to Plotner's, Case's drug-and-book store was the nicest. When you first went in, it smelled of cough candy and orris root, but pretty soon you could notice the smell of drums and new sleds, and about the last smell, (sort of down at the bottom of things) was the smell of new books, the fish-glue on the binding, and the muslin covers, and the printer's ink, and that is a smell that if it ever gets a good hold of you, never lets go. There were the "Rollo" books, and the "Little Prudy" books, and "Minnie and Her Pets," and the "Elm Island" series, and the "Arabian Nights," with colored pictures, and There were skates all curled up at the toes, and balls of red and black leather in alternate quarters, and China mugs, with "Love the Giver," and "For a Good Boy" in gilt letters on them. Kind of Dutch letters they were. And there were dolls with black, shiny hair, and red cheeks, and blue eyes, with perfectly arched eyebrows. They had on black shoes and white stockings, with pink garters, and they almost always toed in a little. They looked so cold in the window with nothing but a "shimmy" on,, and fairly ached to be dressed, and nursed, and sung to. The little girls outside the window felt an emptiness in the hollow of their left arms as they gazed. There was one big doll in the middle all dressed up. It had real hair that you could comb, and it was wax. Pure wax! Yes, sir. And it could open and shut its eyes, and if you squeezed its stomach it would cry, of course, not like a real baby, but more like one of those ducks that stand on a sort of bellows thing. Though they all "chose" that doll and hoped for miracles, none of them really expected to find it in her stocking sixteen days later. (They kept count of the days.) Maybe Bell Brown might get it; her pa bought her lots of things. She had parlor skates and a parrot, only her ma wouldn't let her skate in the parlor, it tore up the carpet so, and the parrot bit her finger like anything.

The little boys kicked their copper-toed boots to keep warm and quarreled about which one chose the train of cars first, and then began to quarrel over an army of soldiers.

"I choose them!"

"A-aw! You choosed the ingine and the cars."

"Dung care. I choose everything in this whole window."

"A-aw! That ain't fair!"

In the midst of the wrangle somebody finds out that Johnny Pym has a piece of red glass, and then they begin fighting for turns looking through it at the snow and the court-house. But not for long. They fall to bragging about what they are going to get for Christmas. Eddie Cameron was pretty sure he 'd get a spy-glass. He asked his pa, and his pa said "Mebby. He'd see about it." Then, just in time, they looked up and saw old man Nicholson coming along with his shawl pinned around him. They ran to the other side of the street because he stops little boys, and pats them on the head, and asks them if they have found the Savior. It makes some boys cry when he asks them that.

The Rowan twins - Alfaretta and Luanna May - are working a pair of slippers for their pa, one apiece, because it is such slow work. Along about suppertime they make Elmer Lonnie stay outside and watch for his coming, and he has to say : "Hello, pa!" very loud, and romp with him outside the gate so as to give the twins time to gather up the colored zephyrs and things, and hide them in the lower bureau drawer in the spare bedroom. At such a time their mother finds an errand that takes her into the parlor so that she can see that they do not, by any chance, look into the middle drawer in the farther left-hand corner, under the pillow-slips.

One night, just at supper-time, Elmer Lonnie said: "Hello, pa!" and then they heard pa whispering and Elmer Lonnie came in looking very solemn - or trying to - and said: "Ma, Miss Waldo wants to know if you won't please step over there a minute."

"Did she say what for? Because I'm right in the midst of getting supper. I look for your pa any minute now, and I don't want to keep him waiting."

"No 'm, she didn't say what for. She jist said: 'Ast yer ma won't she please an' step over here a minute.' I wouldn't put anythin' on. 'T ain't cold. You needn't stay long, only till . . . I guess she's in some of a hurry."

"Well, if Harriet Waldo thinks 'at I haven't anythin' better to do 'n trot around after her at her beck an' . . . . All right, I'll come."

The twins got their slippers hid, and Mrs. Rowan threw her shawl over her head, and went next door to take Mrs. Waldo completely by surprise. The good woman immediately invented an intricate problem in crochet work demanding instant solution. Mr. Rowan had brought home a crayon enlargement of a daguerreotype of Ma, taken before she was married, when they wore their hair combed down over their ears, and wide lace collars fastened with a big cameo pin, and puffed sleeves with the armholes nearly at the elbows. They wore lace mitts then, too. The twins thought it looked so funny, but Pa said: "It was all the style in them days. Laws! I mind the first time I took her home from singin' school. . . . Tell you where less hide it. In between the straw tick, and the feather tick." And Luanna May said: "What if company should come?" Elmer Lonnie ran over to Mrs. Waldo's to tell Ma that Pa had come home, and wanted his supper right quick, because he had to get back to the store, there was so much trade in the evenings now.

"I declare, Emmeline Rowan, you're gettin' to be a reg'lar gadabout," said Mr. Rowan, very savagely. "Gad, gad, gad, from mornin' till night. Ain't they time in daylight fer you an' Hat Waldo to talk about your neighbors 'at you can't stay home long enough to git me my supper?"

He winked at the twins so funny that Alfaretta, who always was kind of flighty, made a little noise with her soft palate and tried to pass it off for a cough. Luanna May poked her in the ribs with her elbow, and Mrs. Rowan spoke up quite loud: "Why, Pa, how you go on! I wasn't but a minute, an' you hardly ever come before halfpast. And furthermore, mister, I want to know how I'm to keep this house a-lookin' like anything an' you a-trackin' in snow like that. Just look at you. I sh'd think you'd know enough to stomp your feet before you come in. Luanna May, you come grind the coffee. Alfie, run git your Pa his old slippers." That set both of them to giggling, and Mrs. Rowan went out into the kitchen and began to pound the beefsteak.

"D' you think she sispicioned anythin'?" asked Mr. Rowan out of one side of his mouth, and Elmer Lonnie said, "No, sir," and wondered if his Pa "sispicioned anythin'" when Ma said, "Run git the old slippers."

Mr. Waldo always walked up with Mr. Rowan, and just about that time his little Mary Ellen was climbing up into his lap and saying: "I bet you can't guess what I'm a-goin' to buy you for a Christmas gift with my pennies what I got saved up."

"I'll just bet I can."

"No, you can't. It's awful pretty - I mean, they're awful pretty. Somepin you want, too." How could he guess with her fingering his tarnished cuff buttons and looking down at them every minute or two?

"Well, now, let me see. Is it a gold watch?"

"Nope."

"Aw, now! I jist set my heart on a gold watch and chain."

"Well, but it'd cost more money 'n I got. Three or fifteen dollars, mebby."

"Well, let me see. Is it a shotgun?"

"No, sir. Oh, you just can't guess it."

"Is it a - a - Is it a horse and buggy?"

"Aw, now, you're foolin'. No, it ain't a horse and buggy."

"I know what it is. It's a dolly with real hair that you can comb, and all dressed up in a blue dress. One that can shut its eyes when it goes bye-bye."

Little Mary Ellen looks at him very seriously a minute, and sighs, and says: "No, it ain't that. But if it was, wouldn't you let me play with it when you was to the store?" And he catches her up in his arms and says: "You betchy! Now, I ain't goin' to guess any more! I want to be surprised. You jump down an' run an' ask Ma if supper ain't most ready. Tell her I'm as hungry as a hound pup."

He hears her deliver the message, and also the word her mother sends back: "Tell him to hold his horses. It 'll be ready in a minute."

"It will, eh? Well, I can't wait a minute, an' I'm goin' to take a hog-bite right out of YOU!" and he snarls and bites her right in the middle of her stomach, and if there is anything more ticklesome than that, it hasn't been heard of yet.

After supper, little Eddie Allgire teases his brother D. to tell him about Santa Claus. D. is cracking walnuts on a flat-iron held between his knees.

"Is they any Santy Claus, D.?"

"W'y, cert, they is. Who says not?"

"Bunty Rogers says they ain't no sech a person."

"You tell Bunt Rogers that he's a-gittin' too big fer his britches, an' first thing he knows, he'll whirl round an' see his naked nose. Tell him I said so."

"Well, is they any Santy Claus?"

"W'y cert. Ain't I a-tellin' you? Laws! ain't you never seen him yet?"

"I seen that kind of a idol they got down in Plotner's winder."

"Well, he looks jist like that, on'y he's alive."

"Did you ever see him, D.?"

"O-oh, well! Think I'm goin' to tell everything I know? Well, I guess not."

"Well, but did you now?"

"M-well, that 'd be tellin'."

"Aw, now, D., tell me."

"Look out what you're doin'. Now see that. You pretty near made me mash my thumb."

"Aw, now, D., tell me. I think you might. I don't believe you ever did."

"Oh, you don't, hey? Well, if you had 'a saw what I saw. M-m! Little round eyes an' red nose an' white whiskers, an' heard the sleigh bells, an' oh, my! them reindeers! Cutest little things! Stompin' their little feet" Here he stopped, and went on cracking nuts.

"Tell some more. Woncha, please? Ma, make D. tell me the rest of it."

Huck-uh! Dassant. 'T wouldn't be right. Like's not he won't put anythin' in my stockin' now fer what I did tell."

"How'll he know?"

"How'll he know? Easy enough. He goes around all the houses evenings now to see how the young ones act, an' if he finds they're sassy, an' don't mind their Ma when she tells them to leave the cat alone, an' if they whine: 'I don' want to go out an' cut the kindlin'. Why cain't D. do it ?' then he puts potatoes an' lumps o' coal in their stockin's. Oh, he'll be here, course o' the evenin'."

"D' you s'pose he's round here now?" Eddie got a little closer to his brother.

"I wouldn't wonder. Yes, sir. There he goes now. Sure's you're alive."

"Where?"

"Right over yan. Aw, you don't look. See? There he is. Aw! you're too slow. Didn't you see him? Now the next time I tell you - Look, look! There! He run right acrost the floor an' into the closet. Plain 's day. didn't you see him? You saw him, mother?"

Mrs. Allgire nodded her head. She was busy counting the stitches in a nubia she was knitting for old Aunt Pashy, Roebuck.

"W'y, you couldn't help but see him. didn't you take notice to his white whiskers ?"

"Ye-es," said the child, slowly, with the wide-open stare of hypnosis.

"Didn't you see the evergreen tree he carried?"

"M-hm," said Eddie, the image taking shape in his mind's eye.

"And his brown coat all trimmed with fur, an' his funny peaked hat? An' his red nose? W'y, course you did." The boy nodded his head. He was sure now. Yes. Faith was lost in sight. He believed.

"I expect he's in the closet now. Go look."

"No. You." He clung to D.

"I can't. I got this flat-iron in my lap, an' wouldn't spill the nut-shells all over the floor. You don't want me to, do you, Ma?"

Mrs. Allgire shook her head.

"Well, now," said D. "Anybody tell you they ain't sich a person as Santy Claus, you kin jist stand 'em down 'at you know better, 'cause you seen him, didn't you?"

Eddie nodded his head. Anyhow, what D. told him was "the Lord said unto Moses," and now that he had the evidence of his own eyes - Well, the next day he defied Bunt Rogers and all his works. To tell the plain truth, Bunt wasn't too well grounded in his newly cut infidelity.

In the public schools the children were no longer singing:

"None knew thee but to love thee,
thou dear one of my heart;
Oh, thy mem'ry is ever fresh and green.
The sweet buds may wither and fond hearts be
broken,
Still I love thee, my darling, Daisy Deane."

They turned over now to page 53, and there was a picture of Santa Claus just as in Plotner's window, except that he had a pack on his back and one leg in the chimney. This is what they sang:

"Ho, ho, ho! Who wouldn't go?
Ho, ho, ho! Who wouldn't go ?
Up on the house-top, click, click, click
Down through the chimney with good St. Nick."

Miss Munsell, who taught the D primary, traded rooms with Miss Crutcher, who taught the "a-b Abs." Miss Munsell was a big fat lady, and she smiled so that the dimples came in both cheeks and her double Chin was doubter than ever, when she told the children what a dear, nice teacher Miss Crutcher was, and how fond she was of them, and wouldn't they like to make a Christmas present to their dear, kind teacher? They all said "Yes, mam." Well, now, the way to do would be for each child to bring money (if Miss Munsell had smiled at a bird in the tree as she did then, it would have had to come right down and perch in her hand), just as much money as ever they could, and all must bring something, because it would make Miss Crutcher feel so bad to think that there was one little boy or one little girl that didn't love her enough to give her a Christmas present. And if everybody brought a dime or maybe a quarter, they could get her such a nice present. If their papas wouldn't let them have that much money, why surely they would let them have a penny, wouldn't they, children? And the children said: "Yes, mam."

"And now all that love their dear, kind teacher, raise their hands. Why, there's a little girl over that hasn't her hand up! That's right, dear, put it up, bless your little heart! Now, we mustn't say a word to Miss Crutcher, must we? No. And that will be our secret, won't it? And all be sure to have your money ready by to-morrow. Now, I wonder if you can be just as still as little mice. I'm going to give this little girl a pin to drop and see if I can hear it out in the hall."

Then she tiptoed down the hall clear to her own room and Mary Ellen Waldo let the pin drop, and Miss Mussell didn't come back to say whether she heard the pin drop or not. The children sat in breathless silence. Selma Morgenroth knocked her slate off and bit her lip with mortification while the others looked at her as much as to say: "Oh, my! ain't you 'shamed ?" Then Miss Crutchet came back and smiled at the children, and they smiled back at her because they knew something she didn't know and couldn't guess at all. It was a secret.

The next morning Miss Crutchet traded rooms again, and the little children gave Miss Mussell their money, and she counted it, and it came to $2.84. The next day she came again because there were three that hadn't their money, so there was $2.88 at last. Miss Mussell had three little girls go with her after school to pick out the present. They chose a silver-plated pickle caster, which is exactly what girls of seven will choose, and, do you know, it came exactly to $2.88?

Then, on the last day of school, Miss Mussell came in, and, with the three little girls standing on the platform and following every move with their eyes as a dog watches his master, she gave the caster to Miss Crutchet and Miss Crutchet cried, she was so surprised. They were tears of joy, she said. After that, she went into Miss Munsell's room, and three little girls in there gave Miss Mussell a copy of Tennyson's poems that cost exactly $2.53, which was what Miss Crutchet had collected, and Miss Mussell cried because she was so surprised. How they could guess that she wanted a copy of Tennyson's poems, she couldn't think, but she would always keep the book and prize it because her dear pupils had given it to her. And just as Selma Morgenroth called out to the monitor, Charley Freer, who sat in Miss Crutchers chair, while she was absent: "Teacher! Make Miky Ryan he should ka-vit a-pullin' at my hair yet!" and the school was laughing because she called Charley Freer "teacher," in came Miss Crutchet as cross as anything, and boxed Miky Ryan's ears and shook Selma Morgenroth for making so much noise. They didn't give anything, though they promised they would.

It was not alone in the day schools that there were extra preparations. The Sunday-schools were getting ready, too, and when Janey Pettit came home and told her Pa how big her class was, he started to say something, but her Ma shook her head at him and he looked very serious and seemed to be trying hard not to smile. He was very much interested, though, when she told him that Iky Morgenroth, whose father kept the One-Price Clothing House down on Main Street, had joined, and how he didn't know enough to take his hat off when he came into church. Patsy Gubbins and Miky Ryan and six boys from the Baptist

Sunday-School had joined, too, and they all went into Miss Sarepta Downey's class, so that she had two whole pews full to teach, and they acted just awful. The infant class was crowded, and there was one little boy that grabbed for the collection when it was passed in front of him, and got a whole handful and wouldn't give it up, and they had to twist the money out of his fist, and he screamed and "hollered" like he was being killed. And coming home, Sophy Perkins, who goes to the Baptist Church, told her that there wasn't going to be any Christmas tree at their Sabbath-school. She said that there wasn't hardly anybody out. The teachers just sat round and finally went into the pastor's Bible class. Mr. Pettit said he was surprised to hear it. It couldn't have been the weather that kept them away, could it? Janey said she didn't know. Then he asked her what they were going to sing for Christmas, and she began on "We three kings of Orient are," and broke off to ask him what "Orient" meant, and he told her that Orient was out on the Sunbury pike, about three miles this side of Olive Green, and her Ma said: "Lester Pettit, I wish't you'd ever grow up and learn how to behave yourself. Why, honey, it means the East. The three wise men came from the East, don't you mind?"

At the Centre Street M. E. Church, where Janey Pettit went to Sunday-school, there were big doings. Little Lycurgus Emerson, whose mother sent him down to Littell's in a hurry for two pounds of brown sugar, and who had already been an hour and a half getting past Plotner's and Case's, heard Brother Littell and Abel Horn talking over what they had decided at the "fishery meetin'." (By the time Curg got so that he shaved, he knew that "officiary" was the right way to say it, just as "certificate" is the right way to say "stiffcut.") There was going to be a Christmas tree clear up to the ceiling, all stuck full of candles and strung with pop-corn, and a chimney for Santa Claus to climb down and give out the presents and call out the names on them. Every child in the Sunday-school was to get a bag of candy and an orange, and there were going to be "exercises." Curg thought it would be kind of funny to go through gymnastics, but, just then, he saw Uncle Billy Nicholson come in, and he hid. He didn't want to be patted on the head and - asked things.

Uncle Billy had his mouth all puckered up, and his eyebrows looked more like tooth-brushes than ever. He put down the list of groceries that Aunt Libby had written out for him, because he couldn't remember things very well, and commenced to lay down the law.

"Such carryin's on in the house o' God!" he snorted. "Why the very idy! Talk about them Pharisees an' Sadducees a-makin' the temple a den o' thieves! W'y, you're a-turnin' it into a theayter with your play-actin' tomfoolery! They'll be no blessin' on it, now you mark."

"Aunt Libby say whether she wanted stoned raisins?" asked Brother Littell, who was copying off the list on the order book.

"I disremember, but you better send up the reg'lar raisins. Gittin' too many newfangled contraptions these days. They're a-callin' it a theayter right now, the Babtists is. What you astin' fer your eatin' apples? Whew! My souls alive! I don't wonder you grocery storekeepers git rich in a hurry. No, I guess you needn't send 'ny up. Taste too strong o' money. Don't have no good apples now no more anyways. All so dried up and pethy. An' what is it but a theayter, I'd like to know? Weth your lectures about the Ar'tic regions an' your mum-socials, an' all like that, chargin' money fer to git in the meetin' house. I tell you what it is, Brother Littell, the women folks 'd take the money they fritter away on ribbons and artificial flowers an' gold an'costly apparel, which I have saw them turned away from the love-feast fer wearin', an' 'ud give it in fer quarterage an' he'p support the preachin' of the Word, they wouldn't need to be no shows in the meetin' house an' they 'd be more expeerimental religion."

Abel Horn (Abel led the singing in meeting, and had a loud bass voice; he always began before everybody and ended after everybody) was standing behind Uncle Billy, and Lycurgus could see him with his head juked forward and his eyebrows up and his mouth wide open in silent laughter, very disconcerting to Brother Littell, who didn't want to anger Uncle Billy, and maybe lose his trade by grinning in his face.

"An' now you got to go an' put up a Christmas tree right in the altar," stormed Uncle Billy, "an' dike it all out with pop-corn an' candles. You're gittin' as bad 's the Catholics, every bit. Worse, I say, becuz they never had the Gospel light, an' is jist led round by the priest an' have to pay to git their sins forgive. But you, you're a-walkin' right smack dab into it, weth your eyes open, teachin' fer Gospel the inventions o' men."

"W'y what, Uncle Billy?"

"W'y, this here Santy Claus a-climbin' down a chimley an' a-cuttin' up didoes fer to make them little ones think they is a reel Santy Claus 'cuz they seen him to the meetin' house. Poot soon when they git a little older 'n' they find out how you been afoolin' 'em about

Santy Claus, they'll wonder if what you been a-tellin' 'em about the Good Man ain't off o' the same bolt o' goods, an' another one o' them cunningly devised fables. Think they'll come any blessin' on tellin' a lie? An' a-actin' it out? No, sir. No, sir. Ain't ary good thing to a lie, no way you kin fix it. How kin they be? Who's the father of lies? W'y the Old Scratch! That's who. An' here you go a - "

The old man was so wroth that he couldn't finish and turned and stamped out, slamming the door after him.

Brother Littell winked and waited till Mr. Nicholson got out before he mildly observed "Kind o' hot in under the collar, 'pears like."

"Righteous mad, I s'pose," said Abel Horn.

"You waited on yit, bub?" asked Brother Littell. "I betchy he's a-thinkin' right now he'll take his letter out o' Centre Street an' go to the Barefoot Church. He would, too, if 't wasn't clean plumb at the fur end o' town an' a reg'lar mud-hole to git there."

"Pity him an' a few more of 'em up in the Amen corner wouldn't go," said Abel Horn. "Mind the time we sung, 'There is a Stream?' You know they's a solo in it fer the soprano. Well, 't is kind o' operatic an' skallyhootin' up an' down the scale. I give the solo to Tilly Wilkerson an' if that old skeezicks didn't beller right out in the middle of it: 'It's a disgrace tud Divine service!' He did. You could 'a' heard him clear to the court-house. My! I thought I'd go up. Tilly, she was kind o' scared an' trimbly, but she stuck to it like a major. Said afterwards she'd 'a' finished that solo if it was the last act she ever done."

"Who's a-goin' to be Santy Claus?" asked Brother Littell, with cheerful irrevelance.

"The committee thought that had better be kept a secret," replied Abel, with as much dignity as his four feet nine would admit of.

"Ort to be somebody kind o' heavy-set, ort n't it?" hinted the grocer, giving a recognizable description of himself.

"Well, I don' know 'bout that," contested Abel. "Git somebody kind o' spry an' he could pad out weth a pilfer. A pussy man 'd find it rather onhandy comin' down that chimbly an' hoppin' hether an' yan takin' things off o' the tree. Need somebody with a good strong voice, too, to call off the names . . . . Woosh's you'd git them things up to the house soon 's you kin, Otho. Ma's in a hurry fer 'em."

"Betchy two cents," said Brother Littell to his clerk, Clarence Bowersox, "'at Abel Horn 'll be Santy Claus."

"Git out!" doubted Clarence.

"'Ll, you see now. He's the daggonedest feller to crowd himself in an' be the head leader o' everything. W'y, he ain't no more call to be Santy Claus 'n that hitchin' post out yan. Little, dried-up runt, bald 's a apple. Told me one time: 'I never grow'd a' inch tell I was sixteen 'n' then I shot up like a weed.' . . . Bub, you tell yer Ma if she wants a turkey fer Christmas she better be gittin' her order in right quick."

Only six more days till Christmas now - only five - only four - only three - only two - Christmas Eve. One day more of holding in such swelling secrets, and some of the young folks would have popped right wide open. Families gather about the Franklin stove, Pa and Ma gaping and rubbing their eyes - saying, "Oh, hum!" and making out that they are just plumb perishing for the lack of sleep. But the children cannot take the hint. They don't want to go to bed. The imminence of a great event nerves them in their hopeless fight against the hosts of Nod. They sit and stare with bulging eyes at the red coals and dancing flames, spurting out here and there like tiny sabers.

The mystic hour draws near. Sometime in the night will come the jingle of silver bells, and the patter of tiny hoofs. Old Santa will halloo: "Whoa!" and come sliding down the chimney. The drowsing heads, fuddled with weariness, wrestle clumsily with the problem, "How is he to get through the stove without burning himself?" Reason falters and Faith triumphs. It would be done somehow, and then the reindeer would fly to the next house, and the next, and so on, and so on. The mystic hour draws near. Like a tidal wave it rolls around the world, foaming at its crest in a golden spray of gifts and love. The mystic hour.

"Oh, just a little longer, just a little longer."

"No, no. You cain't hardly prop your eyes open now. Come now. Get to bed. Now, Elmer Lonnie; now, Mary Ellen; now, Janey; now, Eddie; now, Lycurgus. Don't be naughty at the last minute and say, 'I don't want to,' or else Santa Claus won't come a-near. No, sir."

After the last drink of water and the last "Now I lay me," a long pause . . . . Then from the spare bedroom the loud rustling of stiff paper, the snap of broken, string, and whispers of, "Won't her eyes stick out when she sees that!" and, "He's been just fretting for a sled; I'm so glad it was so 't we could get it for him," and, "I s'pose we ort n't to spent so much, but seems like with such nice young ones 's we've got 't ain't no more 'n right we should do for 'em all we can afford, 'n' mebby a little more. Janey 's ' 'stiffcut' said she was 100 in everything, deportment an' all."

At one house something white slips down the staircase to where a good view can be had through the half-open parlor door. It pauses when a step cracks loudly in the stillness. The parlor door is slammed to.

"D' you think he saw?"

"I don't know. I'm afraid so. Little tyke!"

Something white creeps back and crawls into bed. A heart thumps violently under the covers, and two big, round eyes stare up at the dark ceiling. Somebody has eaten of the fruit of the Tree of Knowledge, and the gates of Eden have shut behind him forever.

He does not sense that now; he is glad in the exulting consciousness that he is "a little kid" no longer. Pretty soon he'll be a man, and then. . . . and then. . . . Oh, what grand things are to happen then!

The mutual gifts are brought out with many a shamefaced: "It looks awful little, but 't was the best I could do for the money. You see I spent more on the children than I lotted to," and many a cheerful fib of: "Why, that's exactly what I've been wishing for." Some poor fools, that have never learned and never will learn that the truest word ever spoken is: "It is more blessed to give than to receive," make their husbands a present of a parlor lamp or a pair of lace curtains, and their wives a present of a sack of flour, or enough muslin to make half a dozen shirts. And there are deeper depths. There are such words as: "What possessed you to buy me that old thing? Well, I won't have it! Now!" The stove-door is slammed open and the gift crammed in upon the coals, and two people sit there with lips puffed out, chests heaving and hearts burning with hate.

It is the truth, but cover it up. Cover it up. Turn away the head. On this Holy Night of Illusion let us forget the truth for once. There are three hundred and sixty-four other nights in which to consider the eternal verities. On this one, let us be as little children. "Let us now go even to Bethlehem and see this thing which is come to pass."

The mystic hour draws nigh. The lights go out, one by one. The watchman at the flax mills rings the bell, and they that are waking count the strokes that tremble in the frosty air. Eleven o'clock. Father and mother sit silent by the fire. The tree in the corner of the room flashes its tinselry in the dying light. A cinder tinkles on the hearth. Their thoughts are one. "He would be nine years old, if he had lived," murmurs the mother. Their hands grope for each other, meet and clasp. Something aches in their throats. The red coals swell and blur into a formless mass.

The mystic hour is come. The town sleeps. The moon rides high in the clear heavens. The wind sighs in the fir trees. Faint and far-off across the centuries sounds the chant of angels.

The hour is come.